I0542319

Heavenly Sins

BETWEEN GOOD AND EVIL

L.M. BROWN

BETWEEN GOOD AND EVIL

Chapter One

Tristan Garrett watched the waves as they lapped closer to his bare feet. Behind him Machidiel and Alastor packed up their belongings and prepared to return to the real world, as Tristan had come to think of it. He'd known from the start their idyllic island holiday wasn't meant to last—he just wished their escape wasn't coming to an end quite so soon.

Resting his chin on his drawn-up knees, he stared at the sinking sun, willing time to stop so he didn't have to go back. Unfortunately, despite all his newly acquired powers, stopping time or turning back the clock weren't amongst them.

He didn't even turn round when Alastor flopped down on the sand beside him.

"Have you thought more about our idea?" Alastor asked. He sounded unsure.

Tristan snorted. He'd thought of little else.

It wasn't that he hated the idea of relocating, though he'd balked at first. No, the idea had a certain appeal to him. He just didn't think living somewhere else would solve his current problem. If it would, he'd be down at the estate agent's first thing in the morning. Unfortunately, no matter where he lived, Lawrence would be able to find him.

Alastor reached around Tristan's shoulders and pulled him into his side. "We'll sort things out, don't worry."

"How?" Tristan asked. "I'm bound to Lawrence for fuck knows how long, and the only way to escape his clutches is to turn some innocent human into a monster like me."

Alastor smacked Tristan's thigh, perhaps a little harder than necessary. "You're not a monster, so stop calling yourself one. Unless you think I'm a monster too?"

Tristan sighed and covered his face.

"Do you?" Alastor asked.

Tristan wouldn't meet Alastor's eyes. Even though he'd known Alastor to be a demon almost from the start of their relationship, he'd never thought of him as a monster.

"Then why do you think of yourself that way?" Alastor pressed. "You might be an incubus now, but you're still you. You're more yourself than I've been since turning demon, because you remember your life before. You're *not* some evil monster."

Tristan didn't know the answer to the question Alastor posed. Maybe it was because Alastor was a different sort of demon—or because he'd never known him as a human. Whatever the reason, Tristan could barely stand to face himself in the mirror, and cringed when he saw the red eyes staring back at him instead of the regular green. He'd seen his full demon form just once and he had yet to work up the nerve to take a closer look.

"Are you guys ready to go home?" Mac called from across the dunes.

Tristan finally lifted his head and glanced over his shoulder toward the angel who'd swept him off his feet so unexpectedly the Halloween before last. If anyone had told him his one-night stand with Mac would've led him here, he'd never have believed them.

Here he was, living with two other men—one an angel, the other a demon—and he couldn't bring himself to regret the direction his life had taken at all.

Even becoming a demon didn't seem quite so bad now the memories of his life had been restored to him. He just wished he could figure out a way to get Lawrence, the demon who'd made him, out of his life without finding another human to take his place. He hadn't yet come to terms with being an incubus, a male sexual predator of the demon world, and now Lawrence expected him to find some unsuspecting human and turn him into an incubus too. He'd be ruining someone's life just to save himself. Actually, he'd be ruining more lives than one, because the new incubus would do exactly what Tristan had done to regain control of his sexual appetite, take the life of the human he fed from. Tristan wasn't sure if he could live with himself if he turned another man into a killer, yet what choice did he have? The alternative would be to join Lawrence for as long as the other demon wanted, and Lawrence wanted forever.

Mac strolled over to Tristan and Alastor and crouched down on the sand. "Tristan, what's the matter? Are you hungry?"

Tristan's cock hardened in his shorts as Mac reached out to pat his leg. If it weren't for the fact Mac and Alastor always managed to turn him on so quickly,

Tristan might have thought the reaction stemmed from his demonic sexual appetite. Honestly, the hunger wasn't the problem right now, though Tristan wasn't one to turn down an offer of sex.

Tristan turned to Mac and pressed their lips together, moaning into the kiss.

"Fuck me, Mac." Tristan sent his thought directly to Mac's mind without breaking contact.

"Alastor, go fetch the lube from the satchel," Mac ordered, as he toppled Tristan backwards onto the sand and yanked off his shorts without ceremony.

Alastor returned in seconds and Tristan felt slick fingers teasing his hole. He shivered as two mouths descended on his nipples, sucking and biting them. He relished the sharp pleasure pain as his lovers marked him as theirs.

Closing his eyes, Tristan wriggled his arse, trying to push down on the fingers that never quite entered him.

"Fuck me," he begged. *"Please, Mac. I need you in me. Now."*

Tristan knew Mac had heard his plea. He was sure his words had made it through to the angel. During the last two weeks he had worked on his telepathic ability almost constantly. He *knew* Mac had heard him. Mac had simply chosen to ignore his plea, at least for the moment.

Alastor's tongue circled his navel as Mac lapped at his balls. Tristan closed his eyes and let them work their magic on his body.

"Relax, baby," Alastor whispered through his mind. Tristan smiled at the demon's pet name for him. Whenever anyone else had given him pet names, Tristan had hated hearing them, yet with Alastor it gave him a feeling of being cherished.

Tristan sighed contentedly as Alastor moved lower, joining Mac at Tristan's crotch, licking at every crevice.

The seawater brushed over Tristan's toes as the tide came in. He moved his feet apart, his heels sinking into the wet sand as he lifted his hips, straining toward the teasing tongues.

Simultaneously, Alastor and Mac each sucked one of his testicles into their mouths and Tristan cried out as he began to shudder with the force of his emotions. He opened his eyes and stared down at the two heads bobbing together between his thighs. They were close enough for Mac's blond hair to tangle with Alastor's dark locks. Tristan's cock stood erect and untouched. The head was purple and already leaked pre-cum.

Mac lifted his head and descended on his erection, swiping the slit with his tongue. Alastor meanwhile had moved in the other direction as he sucked and nibbled on the sensitive skin of his inner thighs.

"You're torturing me," he scolded lightly.

"Ah, but this is such fun, baby," Alastor said telepathically, as he pushed a slick finger into Tristan's arse, with Mac's joining it a moment later.

"More," Tristan begged. "Please."

More was what he got as Alastor and Mac each inserted a second finger.

"Oh *fuck*." Tristan nearly sobbed at the burning pleasure of having his two lovers fingering him so thoroughly.

"Is this too much?" Mac asked. *"I know Alastor has a high pain threshold, but we've never gone this far with you. If you want us to stop..."*

"No." Tristan watched the two heads lift and blue and red eyes stared at him curiously. "This feels good," he assured them.

One of them, he wasn't sure who, crooked a finger and rubbed his prostate. The touch sent him over the edge and cum sprayed his chest as his orgasm tore through him.

"Just good?" Mac teased.

Tristan couldn't even summon the strength to answer mentally. He lay panting on the sand, his lovers' fingers buried in his arse and his softened cock exposed to the elements.

He wanted to stay there forever. He didn't want to return to the rest of the world, not knowing what Lawrence expected of him in the imminent future.

The fingers disappeared and Mac pulled him up and into his arms. "It's okay, Tristan, it'll be all right. We'll sort things out."

Tristan buried his face in Mac's chest. Alastor wrapped himself around the two of them and the three lovers held each other for several long minutes.

Eventually though, they had to leave the island. They washed up in the ocean one last time, Mac gathered their belongings, and the three of them transported themselves home in the blink of an eye.

The time to return to their lives had arrived and they couldn't put reality off any longer.

* * * *

Tristan still wasn't entirely sure he wanted to move out of the house he'd lived in since leaving college. It wasn't that he had any strong ties to the place and he hadn't grown up there, yet it was his home. Eventually though, the sense of his lovers' arguments convinced him that moving away from the town where everyone believed him to be dead might be for the best. With that in mind they went to check out the London penthouse flat Alastor had found for sale.

The estate agent led Tristan and Alastor through the flat, pointing out the highlights. "The kitchen, as you can see, is brand new and everything in it is top of the range."

"*That'll please Mac,*" Alastor communicated to Tristan privately as they wandered over to take in the view from the window.

"Wow." Tristan breathed. "You can see for miles."

Alastor grinned and turned back to the estate agent. "You said there's a rooftop garden?"

The estate agent nodded. "Right this way, sir."

Alastor tugged Tristan along and they followed the woman down the hallway toward the door leading out to the garden.

"*I'm nearly there,*" Mac suddenly spoke in Tristan's mind. A quick glance at Alastor told him he'd heard Mac too. If they could pick up his message he must be in the building or close by.

"Wait a minute," Alastor called after the estate agent.

The woman turned round with a frown.

"Mac's on his way," Tristan explained. "We should wait for him."

"Mac?" asked the woman, confusion evident on her face.

Tristan looked at Alastor, who stared right back at him. Neither of them seemed entirely eager to tell the woman they had another lover. She'd not so much as batted an eyelid as she'd shown them the bedroom, but how would she react to their third?

Before either of them had to break the awkward silence and reply, Mac arrived at the door.

"Hey," Alastor said as Mac approached them then kissed them each lightly on the lips.

The estate agent coughed pointedly. "I take it you're Mac?"

Mac held out his hand for her to shake. "A pleasure to meet you, ma'am."

Alastor snickered at his formality, earning him a sharp smack on the arse from Tristan.

"So, what have I missed?" Mac asked.

"Bedroom and kitchen." Alastor grinned. "I think you'll like both."

The estate agent still appeared a little confused and Tristan had a sneaking suspicion she hadn't quite figured out their relationship yet. Her next words confirmed his guess. "I think perhaps this place isn't what you're searching for," she said sadly, clearly not eager to lose the sale. "There's just one bedroom here."

Mac shrugged and smiled. "That's all we need."

"But..." The estate agent blushed scarlet and fumbled with her papers as the penny dropped.

Tristan bit his lip and ducked his head. He knew their relationship would cause a few raised eyebrows in this posh neighborhood. Gay couples tended to create a few stares down at the supermarket, so a trio of men who made no secret of the fact they shared a bed would be even more gossip-worthy.

Alastor chuckled. "Though we'll be shopping for a bigger bed since Mac hogs the mattress and Tristan hogs the covers."

The estate agent, perhaps realizing she may still get a sale, recovered herself enough to continue the tour.

Tristan had to admit the place seemed ideal. Mac was thrilled with the kitchen and Alastor had already chosen the place to install a new hot tub out in the roof garden. They had also noted the extra-large bathroom, tub, and shower. Tristan loved the tub and could easily imagine himself in it with one of his lovers at his back and the other at his front. The idea of being sandwiched between them made him hard and he had to go step onto the bedroom balcony for some air to recover.

The living area was spacious and neutral enough to be decorated any way they wanted. Tristan ran his hand along the low shelf and the estate agent commented on how the last tenant had previously kept an aquarium there which could be viewed from both the living room and the dining room.

Alastor stood in the dining room and grinned through the gap at Tristan. *"I don't know about you, but I rather like the idea of bending you over the shelf and fucking you silly."*

Tristan blushed and ran his hand along the shelf that appeared to be the ideal height for what Alastor had in mind.

"I can see you like the idea, too," Alastor continued as he ran a hand down the wall.

"I prefer the idea of fucking you over it," Tristan teased.

The estate agent, oblivious to their silent exchange, continued to chatter about aquariums and plug outlets for them.

Mac, who had a fair idea what was going on in Alastor and Tristan's heads, steered their guide back to the kitchen with questions about cupboards.

"What do you think?" Alastor asked. *"I bet Mac could keep her busy for at least ten minutes."*

Tristan ignored Alastor's teasing suggestion. *"I think we should take the place."*

"Really?" Alastor spoke out loud and ducked through the nearby doorway to pull Tristan into his arms. "It's not that we don't like your house, but this would be just fantastic."

Tristan hugged Alastor back and pulled him through to the kitchen. "Yeah, this place will be great. It'll be *our* home."

The estate agent's ears perked up as they caught up with her.

"How soon can we move in?" Mac asked. "Money's no object."

Tristan smiled at those words. While he'd never had the opportunity to say such a thing himself, it sure sounded good coming from Mac.

They were going to move into their new home together and life would be wonderful.

Chapter Two

A week later, after everything had been packed and Tristan had said goodbye to his home, they moved into the penthouse flat some two hundred miles away from anyone he'd ever known.

Mac bustled around the kitchen as he cooked omelets for breakfast on their first morning in their new place. Alastor and Tristan lingered in the bathroom and the sounds of moans coming through the open doorways made the cause of the hold-up clear.

He smiled as he adjusted himself in his jeans. He fully intended to bend at least one of his men over the kitchen table just as soon as they finished breakfast.

"Leaving you out, are they?" a familiar voice enquired politely from behind him. Mac spun round with the pan in his hand and glared at the intruder.

Lawrence lounged at the table, as though he had every right to be there.

"In the future, you'll kindly use the front door, knock, and wait for someone to invite you inside, instead of barging in here," Mac told him in a cold voice that brooked no arguments.

"I don't need your permission to enter," Lawrence argued. "And did you think moving to a new city would stop me finding Tristan?"

Mac turned back to the cooker. "Of course not. We just wanted to make a new home for ourselves, away from the place where Tristan and Alastor don't have to remember my dead body in the bedroom, and where Tristan isn't likely to bump into the family and friends who think he's one of the dearly departed."

Lawrence checked his watch and tapped his fingers on the table "What's taking them so long?" he grumbled.

Mac laughed. "Demon stamina, remember? They won't be much longer. Now, what are you doing here so early in the morning?"

"It's been two weeks since we made our bargain. Surely you haven't forgotten. I'm here to collect Tristan for his first lesson in being an incubus."

"At six in the morning? I thought your kind preyed in clubs and college campuses?"

"Six in the morning here is ten at night on the west coast of the US," Lawrence reminded him. "Which means my lessons with Tristan can start right away."

Mac kept his back to Lawrence as he concentrated on his cooking.

"Can you come back tomorrow?" he asked quietly. "Just give us one day in our new home before you come sweeping in here and ruin things."

Mac studied Lawrence over his shoulder. The demon at least seemed to be considering his request. "What's in it for me?" Lawrence finally asked.

"What do you want?" Mac countered. "And at least make your request reasonable."

"A week alone with Tristan."

Mac shook his head. "I'm not going to bargain Tristan's time without his consent."

Lawrence sat back in his chair and folded his arms across his chest. "Then call him in here and we'll see what he says."

Mac turned to switch on the kettle. Calling Tristan in would put a blight on the day for him, whether he went with Lawrence or not.

The sounds from the bathroom became noticeably louder and Mac could tell Alastor was reaching his peak. Tristan took far longer to come now he was an incubus, at least when he topped one of his lovers.

Alastor gave an impassioned scream, and Mac's cock pressed against his jeans in response to the sound.

Lawrence smirked at him and eyed his crotch appraisingly. "Got a case of blue balls?" he teased. "How about this for a deal? Let me suck you off right now and I'll come back tomorrow for Tristan."

Mac couldn't stop himself recoiling from the demon as he rose from the table and eased his way closer.

"Think fast, angel," Lawrence said, and when he called Mac 'angel', the word wasn't the term of endearment Alastor whispered in his ear at night. Lawrence's sole intention was to insult him.

"Why would you even want to suck me?" Mac asked. "I repulse you as much as you repulse me."

Lawrence placed his hand across his heart dramatically. "You hurt my feelings."

"Why?" Mac repeated. "Tell me why or no deal."

"Because I know you hate the idea," Lawrence explained. "You'd feel guilty, as though you'd betrayed them, and because you don't want them to know I've been here, you'll not tell them what we've done. Which means I have something to keep you in line in the future."

"Blackmail?"

"That's such a dirty word."

"But accurate."

"Quite. So, do we have a deal?"

Mac could hear Tristan and Alastor still going at it and he nodded once. He'd give Tristan one more day to enjoy his freedom. This would be his house-warming gift to him.

He pulled down his zipper and took out his cock. Lawrence sank to his knees in the blink of an eye.

Mac sneered down at the incubus. Did this lower class demon seriously think he could blackmail an angel of Machidiel's age? Tomorrow, when Lawrence returned, Mac would make sure to tell Alastor and Tristan what had transpired this morning. They would understand why he'd made his decision.

He closed his eyes so as not to see the unfamiliar head at his crotch. The demon sucked him roughly, his teeth scraping along his sensitive flesh. Considering Lawrence was an incubus, Mac would have thought he'd have a little more finesse when it came to pleasuring another man.

"What the fuck?"

Mac's eyes flew open and he looked across the room to where Alastor and Tristan stood in the doorway, both naked and with twin expressions of horror on their faces. Lawrence pulled back and turned to the others.

Mac wondered if perhaps Alastor and Tristan wouldn't understand after all.

Alastor moved first. He disappeared from his spot to reappear a moment later right beside them. He yanked Lawrence up by the hair and punched him in the face. "What the fuck do you think you're doing?" he yelled.

Mac didn't take his eyes from Tristan's. *"I can explain."* He sent the words to Tristan alone and breathed a sigh of relief when Tristan nodded and turned to go into the living room.

"I'll join you in a minute." Alastor gestured for Mac to follow Tristan. Mac refastened his zipper and hurriedly departed the kitchen.

"Well?" Tristan asked quietly after Mac had taken a seat on the new, black leather sofa.

"I made a deal with him," Mac explained. "I'd let him suck me off and he'd come back tomorrow to collect you for your first lesson."

Tristan nodded as though he'd suspected that might be the case. "And what would you have done tomorrow?"

Mac studied the bare floor and didn't answer.

"You can't protect me from him forever," Tristan pointed out. "I made the deal with him and I have to fulfill my side of the bargain sooner or later."

"I just didn't want our first day here to be spoiled by him."

Tristan snorted and gave Mac a wry grin. "Yeah, because seeing the slimy little git in there sucking you off won't spoil anyone's day."

"You weren't meant to see us. I thought you and Alastor would be longer in the shower."

Tristan snaked his arm around Mac's waist and rested his head on his shoulder. "We might have been, except we could smell burning in the kitchen and thought we'd better see what had distracted our resident chef."

Alastor strolled into the room and joined them on the sofa with a satisfied smile on his face. "He's gone to lick his wounds. He said he'd be back tomorrow. I've turned the cooker off as well."

Mac turned to Alastor. "Well, aren't you going to say anything about what you saw?"

Alastor sighed and waved Mac toward the door. "Just go take a shower and I'll suck you off when you come back."

"But—"

Alastor shooed him away and Mac hurried to the bathroom, eager to wash away any lingering trace of Lawrence.

By the time he returned, Tristan had salvaged what he could of the burnt omelets and tossed out the rest. Alastor sat perched on the counter, drinking his coffee.

"Are we good?" Mac asked.

"We're *very* good," Alastor answered with a brief grin before his face became stern. "But not if we start lying to each other and sneaking around. Do I need to remind you what happened the last time you kept something from us?"

Mac didn't need any reminder. He'd ended up dead, and it was rather difficult to forget such a thing.

Tristan patted Mac on the arm and poured him a coffee. "Let's just forget about Lawrence for the rest of the day," he suggested. "We've still got some unpacking to do and isn't the hot tub being delivered this afternoon?"

Alastor hopped down from the counter. "Now, Mac, my impulsive angel, I believe I promised you a blow job."

Mac put his coffee to one side and pulled a chair out from the table. He twisted the seat round and sat down. Alastor sank to his knees before Mac had pulled down his zipper and Mac sighed with pleasure as his lover carefully took him into his mouth. Alastor was always cautious of his teeth and Mac gave himself to his lover.

Alastor licked at his penis with far more skill than Lawrence had shown. His tongue teased him mercilessly, stroking his tip as he sucked him.

"You do this so well," Mac praised.

"Better than me?" Tristan teased as he palmed his own crotch from across the table.

"You're both equally good at satisfying me." Mac ran his fingers through Alastor's hair. He wanted to thrust into his lover's willing mouth, yet he knew doing so would probably result in him sliding right off the kitchen chair.

Alastor reached out and cupped his balls, squeezing and fondling them as he closed his eyes and concentrated on his task. Mac smiled at the look of pure pleasure on the demon's face as he sucked him.

Tristan moved round the table and turned Mac's face toward him. Mac met his eyes and he caught the worry in the red orbs. It seemed Lawrence had managed to ruin their first day in their new home after all. He pulled Tristan into the kiss his lover had come to him for. He moaned loudly, sucking Tristan's tongue into his mouth in the same rhythm Alastor sucked his cock.

"If I see Lawrence touch you again, I'll kill him with my bare hands," Tristan said. *"No one is allowed to touch you except us."*

"That goes for me too," Alastor promised. *"You're ours and no other demon, angel or human will ever touch you again."*

Mac didn't break contact with Tristan's lips. *"No one else,"* he agreed. *"Just you."*

Alastor responded to his words by sucking him with renewed vigor. Mac pulled out of Tristan's kiss with a cry of pleasure. His balls tightened and he came in a hot flood into Alastor's mouth.

"*That's it,*" Alastor said. "*Give me everything you have.*"

"*Oh fuck.*" Mac shouted as Alastor's tongue stroked his sensitive flesh and he shivered as a second wave of pleasure ripped through him.

"*No one else but us is allowed to taste you this way.*" Alastor pulled back.

Mac wondered for a moment why he was still communicating telepathically, then he realized his mouth was full with Mac's seed and he wasn't swallowing yet. Mac watched as Alastor stood, turned Tristan toward him and took him into his arms.

The two demons kissed passionately, sharing Mac's essence between them as the angel watched.

"*You always taste so good.*" Tristan sighed and Mac could tell the words were meant for him. "*The taste of you and Alastor together like this is more addictive than any drug. I can't get enough of it.*"

Mac staggered to his feet and moved closer to his lovers. "Everything I have is yours."

Tristan and Alastor parted and two pairs of red eyes gazed at him with nothing but pure lust.

Mac suspected they would be spending most of the day naked and he hoped more than anything they had no more unexpected visitors.

* * * *

Mac woke up as a familiar whispering through his mind pulled him from sleep. Alastor grunted as Mac dislodged him from where he draped over his chest.

"Going somewhere?" Tristan asked from the other side of Alastor.

"I'm being summoned."

"Oh. Are you in trouble?"

"I hope not."

Alastor opened his eyes and gave a small snort. "Raphael probably wants to make sure you haven't been corrupted yet."

"It's not Raphael summoning me." Mac pulled up his jeans. "It's Michael."

"Like there's a difference," Alastor muttered.

Mac suspected Alastor was probably right, but this latest summons worried him. Only two angels had ever summoned him before, Raphael as his direct superior, and Azrael, the angel who had trained him. To be summoned by the archangel Michael, the being often seen as the leader of all the archangels, was unusual and just a little frightening. Mac didn't even finish buttoning his shirt before he disappeared from the room. He didn't want to keep Michael waiting.

As well as being nervous, Mac found his curiosity piqued. Why had he been summoned to the Realm of Angels today?

Angels and newly deceased mortals milled around, going about their business in a hive of activity. Mac had never once seen the realm deserted. No matter how many beings arrived, the realm always had enough room for them all, without being overcrowded. Bathed in permanent sunlight, the main arrival area had been designed to be a classic view of heaven, so as to ease the transition for the newly deceased. Although sitting on the fluffy white clouds wasn't possible, they were there in abundance, giving the realm the appearance of being right up there in the clouds, as opposed to in another dimension.

On his arrival in the main concourse, Mac saw Michael, along with half a dozen or so other angels, congregating to the side. Michael saw him and waved him over. Mac smiled, recalling that of all the archangels, Michael alone seemed to refrain from the pettiness and quarrels running rife through their ranks.

"Thank you for coming so promptly." Michael cast an amused glance at Mac's feet as he approached. "You didn't have to leave your shoes behind though."

Mac glanced down at his bare feet and flushed. "I thought the summons might be urgent."

"Not quite *that* urgent," Michael teased. A couple of the other angels with him chuckled and Mac couldn't help smiling along with them. "Now, are we all here?"

The angels looked around the group, although Mac had no idea if anyone else was expected.

"Just Lailah missing," an angel Mac didn't recognize told them.

"She knows where to find us when she answers," Michael said. "Come on, most of you know the way by now."

Mac followed the group. He felt a little out of step, as though they all knew why Michael had called them except for him. They passed the most common archways and into the area designated for the residences of the angels when they were not on Earth. They had been walking for nearly ten minutes when Michael stepped up to a modest and unadorned archway and waved everyone past him and inside.

"I hope you've got some food in this time," a dark-haired, spritely angel teased as she entered. Mac couldn't contain his surprise at the way she spoke to the archangel. He wondered how she dared. Michael didn't seem to mind. He laughed and nodded.

"What's this all about?" Mac asked as he approached the archway.

"You'll find out in a few minutes," Michael told him. "Not out here."

Mac let Michael nudge him through the archway. Once on the other side Mac found himself in a spacious and airy room, lit from an unknown source.

"Welcome to my home," Michael said from behind him. "Please take a seat."

Mac sat down on one of the large, comfortable-looking chairs. No one else had waited for an invitation from their host.

The angel who had asked about the food sat on the floor, conveniently close to the buffet table that had apparently been laid out for them.

"Please help yourselves to something to eat," Michael offered. "Drinks are in the kitchen if you want one."

Mac wasn't hungry but he followed one of the other angels into the kitchen for a drink.

"I'm Pel." The other angel went directly to the cupboard containing the glasses. Mac had no doubt Pel had been in the kitchen before. The dark-skinned angel with bright green eyes navigated the room with a familiarity a first-time guest couldn't. "Don't look so worried, you're not in trouble or anything."

"How did you know what I was thinking?"

"Because that's what I thought the first time I got summoned to one of Michael's meetings."

"So, you know what this is all about?"

"Oh yeah. This is my sixth, no seventh, meeting."

"What are we here for?"

"I'll let Michael explain. He'll want to start the meeting as soon as possible and there's no point going through everything twice. Water, wine, or juice?"

"Juice, thanks."

"You sure you don't want something stronger?"

"Am I going to need it?"

Pel laughed. "Come on. Let's go join the others. Grab a few glasses and a couple of bottles of wine. I'm sure at least one angel will want a drink before we're finished."

Mac did as Pel suggested and when he returned to the lounge, he saw another angel had joined them. Lailah had finally arrived.

Once everyone had taken their seats and grabbed what food and drinks they wanted, Michael called the informal meeting to order.

"For the benefit of Machidiel and Astra, a short explanation is required."

Mac smiled at the other apparent newcomer, who appeared to be even more nervous than him. Astra tugged at her hair and chewed her lip, her eyes darting around the room as though searching for the emergency exit.

"You're all here because you have one thing in common. Each of you is in a committed relationship with a demon."

Astra squeaked and scrambled back against the wall, fidgeting as though she wanted the floor to open up and swallow her. Mac felt a little disconcerted. Of course Michael knew of his relationship. As an archangel he had been present when Mac had been summoned to deal with the issues surrounding his relationship with Alastor and Tristan. Mac hadn't considered other angels might be in the same position, though he felt a little foolish for his mistaken assumption now he faced the reality.

"As it directly affects you, it is my duty to inform you that Raguel has petitioned the rest of the archangels to vote on whether to forbid relationships between angels and demons."

"Bloody hell," Pel muttered. "I hoped he'd have given up by now. And why so soon? There's normally a hundred years between his wretched petitions. He made the last one just twenty years ago."

Michael raised his hand to forestall the other outraged and disgruntled comments. "Raguel can make the same petition as frequently as he wishes. The reason he has petitioned now, though, is because he believes he has additional support for his request."

"He thought that last time," Lailah said. "Can't he just leave this alone and let us get on with our lives? We're not doing any harm."

Mac felt uneasy as the others voiced their discontent. He didn't believe in coincidences. This petition had been made soon after his relationship with Tristan and Alastor had become the focus of the archangels. Was Raphael the one offering Raguel additional support? He had made no secret of his disdain for demons — and Alastor in particular.

Eventually the grumbles subsided and Michael spoke again. "I'm not at liberty to say how each of the archangels voted on the petitions in the past, nor to speculate on how they might vote this time. I am merely giving you all forewarning that the petition is in the forum again and each of you needs to consider what you will do if it passes."

"What do you mean?" Astra spoke for the first time since the meeting had begun.

Michael gave her a kind smile. "If the petition passes, each of you must choose between your lovers or your wings."

Mac had expected as much. He didn't know about the others, but his choice was an easy one. He valued his lovers far more than his wings and immortality.

Michael caught his eye as the others continued to talk about the unfairness of the situation and the cruelty of Raguel and his supporters in general. *"You appear unsurprised."* Michael's voice whispered into Mac's mind, unheard by the rest of the guests.

"A little surprised, but mostly resigned. I knew Raguel was against such relationships. I just hadn't realized he had the power to end them."

"Not alone, he doesn't. The majority must rule in his favor for relationships with demons to be forbidden."

"Do you think the petition will pass?"

"I don't know. Although it isn't common knowledge, and I'd appreciate you keeping it to yourself, Raphael has always voted against the petition in the past."

"But not now?"

"He's angry, and Raguel's petition may appear to be the solution for what he perceives to be a problem."

"He's going to change his vote because of me, isn't he?"

"I don't know for sure, but it's a distinct possibility."

"So, all the angels you've summoned here today will suffer because of my actions."

"Don't think like that. Never regret loving someone, no matter who they are."

"You approve of relationships between angels and demons?"

"I believe true love is rare and beautiful and should not be discarded because of the prejudices of another."

"You vote against the petition, don't you?"

Michael waited for several long seconds before replying, causing Mac to wonder if he had overstepped the mark with his question. *"I abstain from voting."*

"Why?"

Michael smiled from his seat across the room. *"My vote is always the last one. It has never made a difference to the outcome of the petition."*

"And if your vote did make the difference?"

"I would have to make my choice and follow my conscience." It wasn't an answer to Mac's question, but in his heart he was sure Michael would vote against the petition. Why else would he call these meetings?

After their private discussion came to an end, Mac sat back and observed the other angels. Some of them were angry about the petition, others, once they had had their say, resigned themselves to the reality of their situation, sat back, and chattered.

Pel, who had taken a seat nearby, turned to Mac. "Raphael is your superior, isn't he?"

"Yes."

"How has he taken the news of one of his angels sharing his bed with a demon? No other angel here is under him."

"Really? There's just me?"

"Yes. Most of us are under Metatron, though a few answer to Michael."

"Michael seems to be quite amenable to the idea of relationships with demons."

"He's the most supportive, certainly. He doesn't have to give us warning about the petitions either, yet he always does."

"Why does he do that?"

"So we can have time to make our choice. How did Raphael react to your relationship?"

Mac shifted uncomfortably. "Not too good. He's assigned me the task of saving them."

"Them?"

Mac flushed. "Alastor and Tristan."

"You have two lovers? Are they both demons?"

"They are now, thanks to me."

"What do you mean?"

Mac didn't want to have this conversation, not with a stranger, in a room full of others he had never met before. He decided to keep his reply as vague as possible. "I made a bad choice and Tristan, who was mortal when I met him, paid the price. He's now an incubus."

"That must have been one hell of a bad choice."

"Putting it mildly."

Pel reached over for a bottle of wine and refilled Mac's empty juice glass. "You need something stronger than freshly squeezed oranges."

Mac shook his head as he accepted the drink.

The gathering broke up a short while later, with each of the angels leaving one by one. Mac stood up to leave as well, but Michael's voice in his mind halted his step. *"Machidiel, if I might impose on your time a little longer, please."*

Mac gave a small nod of acknowledgment and began to gather up the plates and glasses to explain leaving his seat to the last couple of lingering angels.

By the time he returned from the kitchen, Michael alone remained.

"Come Machidiel, let's go for a walk." Michael didn't wait for a response as he gestured toward the large open French doors leading out onto a perfect sandy beach.

"Beautiful," Mac breathed as he took in the vista.

"I like it," Michael agreed. "I enjoy walking along the edge of the sea when I have something to think about. It's calm and peaceful and helps me remember that is how angels are supposed to be."

"You always seem calm to me."

"On the outside. Inside I can be in just as much turmoil as the rest of you."

They walked farther down the beach. The ocean waves, unpolluted by mankind, rolled in over the golden sands.

"Machidiel, I've never asked any of the other angels which choice they would make if they had to decide, but I need to ask you."

"I'd choose Alastor and Tristan."

"Good. I thought so, but I had to be sure."

"Why?"

"Tristan is dependent on you and it would not be good for him to lose you."

"I think he'd cope better than Alastor."

"They would each suffer greatly. Had you said you would choose your wings over them, we might have a more serious problem on our hands."

"What sort of problem?"

"It matters not. Now, I would ask one more thing of you. I want you to speak to Raphael and make your peace with him."

"You think I can sway his vote?"

"Maybe. You have always been one of Raphael's favorites. If anyone can persuade him to give demons the right to have the love of an angel, it's you."

Mac thought Michael was ridiculously optimistic. "I'll see what I can do, but I wouldn't hold your breath."

"You need a little more faith in yourself." Michael patted Mac's arm in encouragement. "Now, have you decided what you're going to do about the bargain Tristan made with Lawrence?"

"Not yet."

"You know you can't put it off forever. If Tristan is forced to initiate another human, his victim will feed until he kills, just as Tristan did. It will also kill something in Tristan if this should happen."

"It won't come to that." At least Mac hoped it wouldn't.

"But what if it does?"

"Then I'll do as I did before."

Michael raised an eyebrow. "Do you imagine your lovers will let you sacrifice yourself again?"

"Of the three of us, I'm the only one who can."

"Alastor will do everything in his power to keep from losing you."

"I know."

"You won't be able to fool him again," Michael warned him.

Mac knew that too. "Do you have any other ideas?" Mac asked.

Michael sighed. "No matter what choices you all make, someone will get hurt."

Mac didn't need the foresight of the archangels to tell him that.

Chapter Three

"Keep still," Alastor scolded. "I can't put it in if you keep moving about."

Tristan huffed. "I don't see why I can't just keep wearing shades."

"Because this is England in winter and you look an idiot wearing sunglasses."

Tristan tugged at his hair and ruffled his fringe so the blond locks fell messily into his face. They didn't cover his eyes, the eyes he didn't want to see. He glared at the colored contact lens on Alastor's finger. "I don't like the idea of having something in my eye."

"It isn't in your eye. The lens rests on the fluids."

"That doesn't sound any better to me."

"Once it's in, you won't even be able to tell." Alastor raised his hand and guided the finger with the lens resting on the tip toward Tristan's right eye again. Tristan couldn't help it, his head moved back away from Alastor's finger as fast as the digit approached.

"Maybe an optician should check my eyes first. Maybe they're the wrong sort for contacts."

Alastor chuckled. "I can take you to see one if you want. Though he'll do the exact same thing I'm doing right now. After he's finished freaking out."

"Oh shit."

"I'd erase his memory afterwards."

"No." Tristan knew what having his memory tampered with was like and he wouldn't want to wish that on anyone. Lawrence had meddled with his mind twice and it had been unnerving to have even the smallest loss of time. "I'll stay still."

Alastor gripped the back of Tristan's head gently and held him still while he inserted first one contact lens then the other. Tristan blinked. "See, it's not so bad, and far preferable to having random people freaking out when they catch your eye in the street, especially since you don't have enough control over your powers to make them forget."

"Won't they just assume I'm wearing colored contacts if they see my red eyes?"

"Most will, but every now and again someone will see you for what you are."

Tristan leaned round Alastor to look into the mirror. Green eyes stared back at him, but the color wasn't quite right. The shade was darker than he recalled, at least he thought so.

"We can find some closer to your natural eye color later." Alastor raised a hand and wiped a stray tear from Tristan's cheek. "Don't cry, baby."

"I can't remember exactly what color green my eyes were."

Alastor kissed him softly on the lips. "I remember."

Tristan wrapped himself about Alastor and kissed him back passionately. The part of him that was pure sex demon was well fed and dormant right now. He needed to be held, and for a few blissful minutes able to forget about his problems.

* * * *

Raphael was giving instructions to a newly winged angel when Mac tracked him down. "It's an easy assignment and I'm sure you'll do wonderfully." Mac couldn't remember the last time Raphael had spoken to him in such a kind manner. No, that wasn't entirely true, it had been before he and Alastor had started on their rocky road to friendship. Before he had begun to see Alastor as a person — a lover — instead of the enemy. He wondered if Raphael would ever again look at him without disappointment.

The new angel disappeared in the blink of an eye, returning to Earth for his mission, and Raphael turned to face Mac. "What brings you up here?"

Mac guided Raphael away from the other angels lingering in the area. "I wanted to talk to you." Mac thought it best not to mention his visit with Michael and the other angels.

"About what?"

"My relationship with Alastor and Tristan. I want to know it won't affect our own relationship."

"You have your assignment."

"An assignment you don't believe I can ever complete."

"Are you giving up on your lovers so soon?"

"I never said that."

"Then what's the problem? You have your wings, your assignment, and your lovers."

"I want your respect," Mac said. "I used to have it — or at least I thought I did."

Raphael's expression softened for a moment. "You're one of my oldest angels. I have always been proud of you. I just don't see why you let yourself be tempted by Alastor."

"And Tristan," Mac added.

"Tristan is a different matter entirely. The two of you finding each other has always been inevitable."

"What do you mean?"

"You have met and loved many times in your past lives. Soulmates almost always find each other, one way or another."

"Tristan's my soulmate?"

"Yes."

"How long have you known this?"

"I've always known, as have you, deep in your heart."

Mac felt the truth of his mentor's words.

Raphael smiled sadly. "I once told you Tristan's destiny was to someday become one of us. He would also have been the first angel under your authority."

"But I don't have angels under me."

"You would have, in time, had Alastor not tempted you away from your path."

Mac drew in a deep breath to calm himself. "You cannot blame Alastor for my choices. I altered Tristan's fate, not him."

"Without his interference, you would not have done so."

"You don't know that."

"Of course you wouldn't have."

Mac shook his head. "I love Tristan. With or without Alastor's suggestion, I would have been tempted."

"Everyone comes across temptation at one time or another. Without the demon's encouragement, you would not have altered Tristan's fate."

"Again, you don't know that."

"It matters not. Tristan's destiny has drifted off course, as has your own. He lives as a demon and you are denied the opportunity to teach him our ways as a new angel."

Mac walked away a few paces. He had never imagined he might one day be a mentor to new angels. The idea that Tristan's death would not have been the end of their relationship and the knowledge he could have trained him as an angel tore Mac's heart in two. "How can I set things right?" he asked.

Raphael stepped closer. "Alastor is a lost cause. Tristan can still be saved. Concentrate on him."

"I won't accept Alastor can't be saved."

"There's nothing human left of him."

"That's not true," Mac argued.

Raphael gave a contemptuous laugh. "Care to enlighten me?"

"He has the capacity to love."

"Lust and sex are not love."

"I know the difference."

"Does he?" Raphael asked.

"Yes."

"Are you sure?"

Mac was absolutely positive of that. Alastor's capacity to love was even stronger than Mac's own. "Yes."

"Then you should have no difficulty in saving him."

Mac's wings darkened in frustration. "How am I supposed to save either of them? They're both demons and everyone knows once you turn demon there's no reversal, not even through death."

"There are ways." Mac waited for Raphael to elaborate. "The first demon of his line could reverse the transformation and take back the demon into himself."

"Aka Manah?"

"Yes. Alastor could petition his present master for permission to see his former master. It's unlikely his request would be granted, but if he truly wants to be saved, he could try. He would, of course, have to risk being taken prisoner in the Underworld himself. As for Tristan, in his case you'd need to get him to petition the original incubus, which is a little trickier."

"Why?"

"Because there's some debate as to who that might be. Aka Manah was quite selective about the demons he made and selfish with the knowledge of how to turn a mortal into one of his line. I doubt Alastor even knows how to turn another into his own kind. The incubi, on the other hand, make no secret of how they turn others, sex and blood being the key ingredients, of course. Their numbers grow all the time, more than any other rank of demon. I suspect most incubi, including Tristan and his maker, don't even know the original incubus."

"That could pose a problem."

"Quite. Of course, if your lovers are truly good and not evil, they won't be wanted in the Underworld and saving them will simply be a matter of time."

"You mean they could simply be thrown out of the Underworld and become mortal?"

"Nothing is ever quite so easy when it comes to demons."

"I don't understand. Can they become human again or not?"

"Anything is possible." Mac suspected Raphael enjoyed being deliberately evasive. "You should probably return home. Lawrence—a thoroughly

unpleasant demon, who was an equally vile human —
will be coming to collect soon."

Mac didn't need the reminder. "Now there's a
demon I could cheerfully send right down to Hell."

"For as long as his bargain with Tristan remains,
even the Underworld cannot hold him. He'll have the
power to find Tristan, no matter where he is."

"We need to find a way to break the bargain before
any more lives are destroyed."

Raphael nodded solemnly. "At least you seem to
have your priorities back into some sort of sensible
order."

Mac wasn't sure if peace had been made with
Raphael or not when he returned home a short while
later. He thought maybe things were better than they
had been before their talk, but he honestly didn't
know if their relationship could ever be entirely
repaired.

* * * *

"This can't be good." Alastor sat at the dining-room
table. Tristan took a seat opposite him and Mac
slipped into his place at the head of the table. Alastor
stretched out his leg and rubbed Mac's shin with his
foot.

Mac shivered and tried to control his body's reaction
to the not-so-innocent touch. "Alastor, stop it."

"What's he doing?" Tristan asked as he slouched in
his seat. Mac suspected he was trying to maneuver his
own foot in the direction of Alastor's crotch. The table,
unfortunately, was too wide for him to reach and was
precisely why Mac had called them into the dining
room in the first place. He wanted a serious discussion
with them, one that didn't involve playing footsie and

groping. Not that he imagined either of his lovers would be inclined to do anything of the sort when they heard what he had to say.

Before Mac could answer Tristan's question, the young demon slid off the chair and landed in a heap on the floor. "Are you finished?" Mac asked politely.

Tristan scrambled to his feet and sat back in his place while Alastor snickered. "Yes."

"Good. Now, I wanted to talk to you about our current problem with Lawrence."

Alastor grimaced. "Can we not talk about him?"

"We have to talk about him sooner or later," Mac pointed out. "And since he plans on coming back for Tristan tomorrow morning, there isn't much time left."

"Maybe Alastor scared him off for a bit?" Tristan suggested. He cast a hopeful glance at each of his lovers before his face fell when reality set in. "Fine. He'll be here at the crack of bloody dawn."

"Quite." Mac looked away from Tristan and Alastor and focused on the modern art painting on the opposite wall. The picture wasn't to his taste at all, but it gave him something to concentrate on.

"What is it?" Alastor asked.

Mac didn't face them as he spoke. "For Tristan to be released from his bargain, he needs to find another human to take his place. That human, to regain control of his hunger, will have to take a life."

"Well, thanks for the recap," Tristan muttered. "I've been trying not to think about it."

Mac met Tristan's eyes and leaned over to take his hand. "Unfortunately, we have to think about it."

"I don't see why we can't just kill Lawrence and put an end to this nonsense that way," Alastor suggested.

"I'd be happy to rip his head off just as soon as you give the word."

Mac glared at Alastor. "Violence is never the answer."

"Seems like a good solution to me," Alastor said. "How about we vote on it? All in favor of me putting Lawrence out of his misery raise your hands now."

Alastor lifted his hand. "Tristan, you know this is the best option."

"Mac's right." Tristan shifted uncomfortably in his seat. "No one else has to die. Besides, how do you know that'll kill him?"

Alastor lowered his arm. "I don't know, but it'll make me feel a lot better."

Mac banged his fist on the table. "No one is killing anyone."

"Apart from whoever I have to pick to turn into a demon," Tristan reminded him. "And whoever he kills after he turns."

"He doesn't have to kill anyone," Mac answered calmly. "If you chose the right man, we could invite him to move in here with us."

"Excuse me?" Tristan asked. "What exactly are you suggesting? That we turn this threesome into a foursome or something?"

"If we have to." Mac frowned, appearing no happier about the idea than he was.

"And what about when this man turns?" Tristan asked. "How do you plan to help him control his hunger?"

"He's going to sacrifice himself again," interrupted Alastor, his voice tight with barely suppressed fury. "He's going to give up his wings and let someone else fuck him to death, just as he did with you."

"No," Tristan shouted and he jumped up from the table. "You can't do it. Not again."

"I have to. Of the three of us, there's only me who can."

"And what about afterwards?" Alastor asked. "Do you think the archangels will just let you give up your wings, sacrifice yourself, and send you back to us *again*?"

"Any angel can give up his wings," Mac said. "The archangels have no say in that, nor in what I do when I'm human again."

"But they can keep you from returning to us when you die," Tristan reminded him. "No, I won't let you do this."

"I can't sit by and let someone else die when I can prevent it," Mac stated firmly. "I'm not telling you this so you can talk me out of it. I'm telling you so you can be prepared. I still hope we can find a way to break the bargain without anyone being turned into a demon, but if the worst happens, this is our one option."

"I don't like this option. You can't make me watch you die again. Once was bad enough. Twice would—" Alastor's voice cracked and tears formed in his eyes.

Mac jumped up from the table and hurried to Alastor's side. "Don't cry," he begged.

"You're asking me to watch you die again," Alastor sobbed. "I can't do that. I can't. I can't."

Tristan joined them and wrapped his arms round Alastor. "I won't let him do this. I'll find a way to break the bargain or I'll die trying."

Alastor sniffled. "Watching you dying wouldn't be any better than watching Mac."

"I'll break the bargain, I swear it." Tristan crossed his heart and gave them a weak smile.

"And if you don't?" Alastor asked. "Mac's idea of making the three of us four is all well and good, except that fourth will be tied to Lawrence instead of you, which means he'll still be in our lives. Not to mention there's no guarantee Mac will even be here if he's killed again."

"I don't want a fourth," Tristan admitted. "Finding someone to turn won't fix this. It'll only make things worse. I'd spend the rest of eternity trying to undo Lawrence's influence over someone else and trying to make sure no one else is hurt in the process. For as long as I'm tied to Lawrence or someone else of my choosing is, it won't be over. I want this done, finished. I'll find a way to break the bargain."

"And how do you intend to do that?" Alastor asked. "Because I sure as hell don't know."

"Me neither," Tristan admitted. "But I'll find a way, I swear I will."

Mac remained silent. He'd made his position clear to his lovers in what he intended to do. He hoped sacrificing himself wouldn't be necessary, but he suspected Lawrence would make it so. Lawrence wasn't going to let Tristan go without a fight, and demonic bargains weren't easily broken.

They needed to do something fast, because if Raguel's petition passed, Mac would no longer have his powers and Lawrence would be certain to take advantage of the fact. He wondered if he should tell his lovers about the petition, but swiftly decided against doing so. They had enough to worry about without adding to their concerns.

Chapter Four

"Where are we?" Tristan asked Lawrence, as he studied the dingy alleyway. It took a moment for his eyes to adjust to the darkness of night, when a few seconds ago he'd been in daylight. He could smell the rotting waste in the dumpster just across from them and wrinkled his nose in distaste.

"Los Angeles. Breakfast time in England is party time over here."

Tristan followed Lawrence as he led the way out onto the street. "Why couldn't we just do this tonight in London or something?"

"Because I wanted to start as soon as possible."

Tristan huffed and hurried after the demon. The sooner he got this over with, the better. "So, what are we going to do tonight?"

Lawrence pointed toward a building a little way up the road. A few people lingered outside, although Tristan couldn't tell if they were queuing or merely hanging around outside the club.

"A nightclub?"

"Yes."

Tristan smiled. At least in LA there might be a chance of seeing someone famous out at night. Then again, he reconsidered as he saw the dive of a club. No one even remotely famous would be likely to hang out at this dump.

Lawrence stopped and turned to Tristan. "Lesson one— How to get in without paying."

Tristan folded his arms and looked at the entrance. "Make myself appear in there."

Lawrence rolled his eyes skyward. "You can only transport yourself to a place you can visualize. And a busy club isn't a good place to just pop into. Too big a risk of being seen appearing."

"Oh yeah. I forgot that." Tristan jerked his head back the way they had come. "So, you found it rather easy to visualize the alley. Hold some fond memories, does it?"

Lawrence ignored him. "You need to learn how to flirt with mortals to get what you want."

Lawrence's patronizing tone grated on Tristan's nerves, which didn't bode well for the evening since the night had barely begun. "I seem to recall my flirting scored me more free drinks than *you* ever managed."

"I'm not talking about regular flirting. I'm talking about using your powers to push people into doing what you want. Any demon can do it, some more proficiently than others. Despite what I think of him personally, Alastor is an expert at mind manipulation. It's his greatest demonic talent, in fact. The one difference between our powers and his is the sexual aspect."

"Why don't you like Alastor?" Tristan asked. "Apart from the fact I chose him over you, I mean."

"That's not enough?"

"You hated him well before then. I'm just curious."

Lawrence seemed to be considering the question before he eventually shrugged. "No real reason. Demons usually work alone and he's a cocky bastard at the best of times." Lawrence turned back to the club. "Watch what I do carefully. Next time I'll expect you to do the same. Oh, and you'll need this."

Lawrence shoved a wad of American money into Tristan's palm before he stalked toward the door. Tristan followed and waited for some great display of demonic powers. In fact all he saw was a bit of over-the-top flirting, insincere flattery, and the bouncer stepping aside to let them in. A hand ran over Tristan's arse as he stepped past and he turned to see the bouncer wink at him suggestively. Tristan suspected he might have got them in for free without any sort of demonic help.

Tristan stared around the club, feeling the momentary wonder at being in an actual Los Angeles nightclub dissipate as he took in his surroundings. The place didn't seem much different from the clubs in England. Hell, it looked in a worse state than many he'd been in over the years. The floor was sticky underfoot, causing Tristan to wonder when it had last been properly cleaned. Empty glasses covered every surface and no one seemed to be bothered about collecting them. He wasn't sure what the American regulations were about the number of patrons in a bar, but he had a feeling if this place had been in England and inspected by the Fire Service, they'd be shut down in an instant.

"Angel at the bar," Lawrence whispered into his mind.

"How can you tell?" Tristan asked out loud. Communicating telepathically with Alastor and Mac had become second nature to Tristan, yet it still felt like an intrusion in his mind when Lawrence spoke to him in that manner.

"The same way any demon can pick out an angel. Just focus on him and you'll see what I mean."

Tristan stared at the man at the bar curiously. He couldn't see what was so different about him. It wasn't as though he could tell Mac was an angel just by looking at him either. "I don't see anything," he finally muttered.

"It's bloody obvious," Lawrence complained. *"And stop talking out loud when you're on the job."*

"On the job?" Tristan snorted. *"I still don't see what gives him away. I never see anything different about Mac either, nor does Alastor."*

"I'm sure Alastor can pick out an angel in the crowd if he tried."

"He couldn't tell Mac had lost his wings when I first turned."

"He probably wasn't looking properly. If Alastor tries, he can see what all demons see when they're scanning for angels. Or in the case of Mac when he lost his wings, he'd have seen what was missing. Though I suppose Mac could have had help keeping his mortal status from you both. Most angels don't bother to hide what they are. If anything, they flaunt it."

Tristan walked up to the bar and waited for the bartender to serve him. If he was going to make it through tonight without strangling Lawrence, he would need plenty to drink.

He studied at the angel at the end of the bar and the second he caught his eye, he saw what Lawrence had been talking about. Just for a moment he glimpsed the heavenly glow surrounding him. A pure white light Tristan ached to reach out and touch. "Oh."

The angel lifted his glass in a silent salute to Tristan. Did he know what he was? Or was he just acknowledging him like he would any other man in the place?

Tristan didn't know, nor did he want to find out. He ordered a beer and moved toward the booths at the other side of the dance floor. He gazed about the place with vague interest. The club didn't appear to cater just to the homosexual community, though there were a few same-sex couples in the place.

"Picked someone yet?" Lawrence interrupted his thoughts again.

Tristan scowled and turned away to watch the dancers.

"I'm not asking you to choose someone to turn tonight," Lawrence continued. *"Just find someone to feed from."*

"I don't need to feed. I made sure of that before I left."

"I don't care. You need to get into the habit of fucking other men."

"I don't want to fuck any men except Alastor and Mac."

Lawrence slammed his glass down on a nearby table. *"It doesn't matter what you want. You're an incubus and you're going to have to start fucking around if you ever plan on finding someone to take your place at my side."*

Tristan ignored him. He wasn't sure which option was worse. He didn't want to be bound to Lawrence, prowling clubs and bars with him night after night. Yet neither did he want to be responsible for inflicting this curse on someone else.

"Will you just pick some bloke to fuck?" Lawrence insisted.

Tristan ground his teeth and studied his beer. *"Can you at least try to understand how difficult this is for me? You're asking me to find someone to cheat on Mac and Alastor with."*

"They know you're going to have sex with other men when you come out with me."

"That's not the point. I don't want to cheat on them. I love them."

Lawrence huffed and snatched Tristan's drink from him. *"Are you forgetting that after just one night with Mac, you spent a year whining about how badly you wanted him again, yet it took all of an hour for you to spread your legs for Alastor when he turned up on your doorstep?"*

"It wasn't like that. You're making what we shared sound cheap and dirty."

"It was cheap and dirty." Lawrence smirked at him and tapped his temple, subtly reminding Tristan he had once had access to all his memories. He might not be able to remember the details now, but it made little difference. Back when Tristan had met Mac and Alastor he had still considered Lawrence a friend — his best friend — and had confided in him accordingly. *"He fucked Mac right out of your mind in a single night."*

"You're missing my point. I love them and I don't want anyone else."

"No, you're missing my point. You're an incubus and you're going to fuck other men when you're out with me."

Tristan spun away, swaying on his feet a little. He wished he'd managed to finish his breakfast before leaving. It seemed strange to be out clubbing at such an odd time.

He stumbled onto the dance floor and lost himself in the pulsing beat of the music. He remembered a time when he and Lawrence had danced together, enticing men they wanted to pull, reeling them in like fish on a line. The last time they had done it had been when Tristan had wanted to draw in Alastor, but pulled Mac instead. It had been the night his life had changed forever. No man could ever match up to Mac, at least until Alastor had arrived on his doorstep a year later.

He glared at Lawrence, warning him to stay away from him tonight. If he did go through with this, it wasn't going to be with Lawrence.

Hands brushed his hips and arse, and he pushed into them blindly. The crush of bodies was sweltering and eventually he stepped away to fetch another drink.

When he reached the bar, he realized he'd had an audience in the form of a bright-eyed youth. The man didn't appear to be as old as Tristan. He suspected he was barely old enough to drink. He had light brown hair that caught the lights from the dance floor as he sat tapping his foot to the music. Despite his reservations, Tristan felt his body react to the open appraisal he saw in the man's eyes. He smiled and waited for him to realize he'd been caught staring.

An innocent blush spread across his admirer's face. Tristan found it quite endearing.

"Like what you see?" asked Tristan, his voice slightly croaky as he tried, and failed, for casual and flirtatious.

"Oh yeah." The youth stuck out his hand. "I'm—"

"No." Tristan cut him off. "I don't want to know your name."

The hand dropped and the young man turned away, clearly embarrassed. "Sorry, I thought…"

The guilt made Tristan's stomach churn. "Sorry. I'm being rude. I'm Tristan."

"You're English?"

Tristan nodded, although he didn't really need to. His accent gave him away as soon as he uttered a word.

"Can I buy you a drink?"

Tristan shook his head. "Let me. What are you drinking?"

"Just a beer, thanks."

Tristan ordered their drinks and they moved to a recently vacated booth near a doorway leading to the toilets, grabbing the seats just ahead of another couple. Tristan sipped from his bottle as he wondered if he could go through with this. He'd talked everything through with Mac and Alastor, and he knew what he had to do — he just didn't know if he could actually follow through.

It didn't help that the one time Tristan had had sex with a mortal since becoming an incubus, he had killed his lover. Mac, the lover in question, had assured him the same thing wouldn't happen again so long as Tristan retained control of his sexual appetite by feeding on a daily basis. Mac had explained his death had been inevitable and the only way to give Tristan back any control at all. Until he had taken a mortal life, he would be unable to stop feeding at all. Mac's sacrifice had ensured Tristan wouldn't take an innocent's life while he was unable to stop himself.

Still, it didn't make things any easier now, knowing that for the first time he would be having sex with someone who he could actually kill if he went too far.

Oblivious to Tristan's inner turmoil, the young man chattered away, asking questions about England and listening intently to Tristan's stilted replies. All the time Tristan wondered whether he could lead him through the door behind him and into the gents without losing the contents of his stomach.

Eventually, during a lull in the conversation, Tristan turned to the youth who had been hanging onto his every word for nearly an hour casually asked, "Want to shag?"

The man frowned at him, his face clouded with confusion for a moment, before he realized what Tristan had asked him. He blushed. "Are you staying somewhere nearby?" he asked, a hopeful note in his voice.

"No, just passing through. Come on." Tristan stood up and gestured toward the doorway. He didn't look to see if his admirer followed behind him—he knew he would.

The toilets appeared to be as dirty as any in an English club and Tristan headed to the cubicle at the far end. The outer door closed behind them, leaving them alone in the small confined space.

"Turn round," Tristan ordered. "And drop your trousers."

He obeyed immediately and Tristan considered the exposed arse without interest. His penis barely even twitched at the sight.

He'd just get this over with as soon as possible. Tristan yanked down his zipper and reached into his underpants to free his still-soft cock. He rubbed the flesh several times until he finally began to harden.

"Spread your legs." Tristan reached down to part the cheeks and guided his length to the young man's entrance. His erection started to wilt when he realized the youth shook a little and he halted his movements. "Have you ever done this before?"

His companion answered with a tiny shake of the head.

"Sex in the toilets of a club, or sex at all?" Tristan questioned.

"At all."

Tristan groaned and stepped back. Fuck. He couldn't do this. Not with him, not like this. He tucked himself back into his trousers and zipped himself up. "Get dressed."

"What?"

Tristan turned away and leaned against the wall. "Just get dressed and get out of here."

"I don't understand."

Tristan sank down onto the floor, his head in his hands. "I can't do this. I thought I could, but I can't."

"Oh. Is it your first time, too?"

Tristan laughed. "Fuck, no."

The youth frowned at him. Tristan gestured for him to take a seat on the floor with him. "Oh fuck, what *is* your name, kid?"

"Cody Hammond, and I'm not a kid."

"Well, Cody, it's nice to meet you. And for my good deed of the day, I'm going to give you some free advice."

Cody sat down.

Tristan sighed. "I know you probably think being a virgin is a bad thing, and you're desperate to get laid, but wait for the right guy."

"How do you know you're not the right guy for me?" Cody asked.

Tristan shook his head sadly. "The right guy will ask your name before he asks you to spread your legs for him. He'll take you home or at least to a hotel rather than into a cubicle in the gents. He'll have lube and condoms and he'll make the sex good for you because he'll care about giving you pleasure."

"I have condoms," Cody interrupted.

"And they're fucking useless in your pocket when my dick's up your arse. You shouldn't have let me go as far as I did without insisting I use one."

"I guess I got carried away."

"Yeah, it's easily done. Don't worry, I'm clean and I never got inside anyway, but next time you might not be so lucky. You can't let yourself get carried away when your safety's on the line."

Cody took in Tristan's advice. "So, can we start again? Maybe see if you're the right guy after all?"

Tristan smiled. "I'm not the right guy for you. I already have two guys and they're more than enough for me."

"You were going to cheat on two other guys with me?" Cody stared at him with wide eyes, as though he couldn't believe what he'd heard. He sounded appalled for the first time since they had met.

"They know I'm here."

"They know about each other?"

Tristan laughed. "Oh yeah. They knew each other before they met me. We all live together."

"You mean..." Cody lowered his voice to a whisper, even though they were alone. "Like in a threesome?"

Tristan opened his mouth to confirm Cody's guess when he heard the outer door open and close.

"Tristan? I know you're in here. Have you fucked him yet?"

Cody's brow furrowed slightly. Tristan drew his finger up to his lips to signal for him to stay quiet.

"Fuck off, Lawrence. I'm not done yet."

Lawrence's steps drew closer. "You're not having sex in there, it's too quiet."

"What part of 'fuck off' don't you understand?"

"What part of find someone to fuck don't *you* understand?" Lawrence countered impatiently. "Either get on with it or get back out here and pull someone else. Because if you think you're going to spend the next ten hours hiding out in the loos, you've got another thing coming. And the sooner you screw someone, the sooner I let you go home to your fuck buddies."

Cody appeared more and more confused and Tristan didn't blame him.

"For crying out loud, Tristan, you're a bloody incubus, act like one and fuck him."

Tristan closed his eyes, wondering just when Lawrence had decided not to bother with secrecy. *"Do you realize how much you're scaring this guy?"* he asked Lawrence silently.

"Then wipe his mind when you're done. Do I have to think of everything for you?"

Tristan wondered whether he should point out to Lawrence he had no idea how to do that particular trick yet.

Cody edged away toward the door, though there was barely any room for maneuver.

Tristan reached out to place a calming hand on Cody's leg. "Cody, it's okay. I'm not going to hurt you."

Cody stopped moving, though his complexion remained pale. "What did he mean when he said you're an incubus?"

"An incubus is a male demon who feeds through sex."

"Oh."

Tristan gave a humorless laugh. "Not the answer you expected — or just something you didn't want to know?"

"Both. Is it true?"

"Do you really want to know?"

Cody shook his head. "I think I'd rather live in ignorance."

Tristan grinned. "Good choice. Now, I don't know about you, but I want to get out of here."

Lawrence banged loudly on the cubicle door. "Tristan, if you're thinking of double-crossing me, you'd better think again."

Tristan climbed to his feet and opened the door. Lawrence's arm was raised to hit the door again. "You are *really* starting to piss me off."

Lawrence yanked him by the arm and dragged him out of the cubicle. "What the fuck is your problem? I'm offering you any bloke you want, you choose this pathetic example, and then you can't even manage to do him."

"Hey." Cody stepped forward and glared at Lawrence. "Who are you calling pathetic?"

Lawrence waved his hand in dismissal and Cody froze in place, trapped within his own body. Tristan knew the ability to freeze someone was within his capabilities. As a newly woken incubus, he had frozen Alastor when he'd tried to stop him from draining Mac to death. He hadn't tried to do the same thing again and considered it a terrible power to have. From the casual way Lawrence wielded the power, he clearly didn't share Tristan's opinion.

Tristan pushed Lawrence up against the wall. "Unfreeze him *now*."

"Why don't you?"

"You froze him."

"As an incubus, you have the power to undo my magic."

"Unfreeze him. Wipe his memory. Then let him leave." Tristan punctuated each demand by banging Lawrence up against the wall.

Lawrence laughed loudly. "He's your problem, so your final lesson for the evening is for you to sort him out."

With that, Lawrence vanished from Tristan's grasp, leaving him alone with the frozen Cody.

Tristan ran his hands through his hair and risked a glance at the young American. *What the fuck was he going to do now?*

"Mac, Alastor, I really need you guys here. I've no idea how to do this."

Unfortunately, his lovers were an ocean and a continent away and had no chance of hearing his plea.

He could feel Cody's gaze on him as he paced the small room, trying to concentrate on unfreezing him with no success at all.

The sounds of movement outside the door signaled his time had run out and Tristan did the one thing he could think of—he took hold of Cody's arm and transported them both back to the penthouse.

C h a p t e r   F i v e

Alastor knelt on the living room floor amidst a tangle of wires as he attempted to set up the flat-screen television and DVD player. Considering he could barely manage to work the remote control, Tristan wondered why he hadn't waited for him to get back and set it up. Alastor didn't see Tristan at first and he cleared his throat to get his attention.

"Hey, baby, back already?" Alastor greeted him as he set aside the tangled mess of cables. "Oh. You brought a guest back? Was that part of the deal?"

"Not exactly," Tristan answered. "Lawrence took off after freezing him and I had to get him out of there before someone saw him. Can you fix him?"

Alastor shook his head slowly. "Freezing someone in their place isn't one of my powers. It's something mainly limited to the incubi. They use it in cases of someone walking in on them while they're feeding."

"He didn't wipe his mind either," Tristan said. "He said I had to do it. Except I don't know how."

Alastor stood and walked over to Cody to study him. "You don't have the ability to modify memories yet. It takes at least a hundred years of practice to manage such a feat with any proficiency."

"Lawrence said I could."

Alastor snorted. "In case you hadn't realized yet, Lawrence is a liar. Now, how about you go fetch Mac from the garden and see if he has any ideas on how to get your young man mobile again."

Tristan walked toward the entrance to the roof garden. "He's not my young man," he muttered.

He left Alastor circling Cody and went in search of Mac. It didn't take long to find his other lover, who was clearing away the rubbish that had gathered on the roof while the property remained empty.

Mac dropped the bag of rubbish as soon as he saw Tristan and rushed to his side. "Tristan, love, what's happened?"

Tristan let Mac hold him in his arms for a minute before leading him back into the penthouse. "I really screwed up and I don't know how to fix it," he confessed as he gestured to Cody.

Mac held his hand they approached the frozen man. "Hmm, well, there's something you don't see every day. Why did you freeze him?"

"I didn't," Tristan replied. "Lawrence did it and told me to reverse it. Except I don't know how."

"Well, you certainly have the ability," Mac confirmed. "You can freeze anyone, including me and Alastor if you wish. Have you tried to undo it?"

"Of course I have. It didn't work, probably because I don't know what I'm doing."

Alastor rubbed at the back of his neck and grinned. "I guess bribing you with sex won't work with this sort of power."

Tristan gave him an irritated look. "How did you manage to unfreeze when I did this to you?" he asked.

Alastor shrugged. "The magic just wore off after you passed out."

"Oh."

"Want me to track down Lawrence and beat the shit out of him?" Alastor asked with over-the-top enthusiasm. He rubbed his hands together in eager anticipation.

"You don't have the power to track him down any more than I do," Mac pointed out. "Besides, violence is never the answer."

Tristan turned to Mac hopefully. "Any suggestions?"

Alastor chuckled. "We could put him out on the roof and use him as a garden gnome."

Tristan poked Alastor in the ribs with his elbow and glared at him. "You're not helping."

"Raphael," Mac suddenly shouted, causing both Tristan and Alastor to jump back startled.

The archangel appeared almost immediately and Tristan wondered if he'd been watching the events of the last few hours. Whether he had or not, he didn't seem pleased to be there. He glared at each of them in turn, his gaze finally resting on Mac.

"Machidiel." The single word was cold and sharply spoken.

"We have a problem," Mac explained, as he waved vaguely toward Cody.

Raphael appeared bored. "So I see. And is that any reason to summon me so rudely?"

Mac dropped down to one knee and bowed his head. "Forgive me, Archangel."

Raphael gestured for Mac to stand and stepped closer to consider the frozen form of Cody. "He appears to be aware of us and his surroundings," he commented.

"We know that," Alastor muttered. "We want to know how to unfreeze him so we can put him back where he came from."

"The incubus has the power to do what you say."

"So everyone keeps saying," Tristan complained. "I just don't know how."

Raphael appraised him coolly. "Then it's about time you did."

"Raphael, great archangel," Mac murmured. "Please could you restore him?"

Raphael didn't seem appeased by Mac's groveling. "No."

"Can't or won't?" Alastor questioned.

Raphael turned to glare at the older demon, disgust clear in his eyes. "Won't."

"Please," Tristan begged. "I can't just leave him like this."

Raphael stepped back. "I am not your master. You're asking the wrong person for help."

"Lawrence refused to undo what he did," Tristan pointed out. "I don't even know where he is."

Raphael closed his eyes for a few moments. "He's in Chicago, feeding from one of his favorites. I can send you to him if you wish?"

Tristan didn't see the point in speaking to Lawrence. "He won't undo it anyway."

"Then if your master won't, perhaps your mutual master will."

"What do you mean?"

Raphael huffed a sigh of impatience. "Your king has the power to reverse Lawrence's magic. I would suggest you petition him to assist you."

With those parting words of advice, Raphael vanished from the room.

"Well, that was helpful," Alastor muttered. "And did anyone else form the impression he doesn't like me?"

"You *are* a demon," Mac pointed out. "Most archangels would kill you on sight."

"He didn't sneer at Tristan as though he'd just crawled out from under a rock."

Tristan sat down on the arm of the sofa as Alastor continued to grumble. Finally he snapped at him. "Are you going to stand there moaning all day, or are you going to take me to the Underworld?"

Alastor halted his complaining. "You need to change first."

Tristan picked at the clothes he had chosen to go clubbing in. "What do you suggest?"

"I don't mean your clothes," Alastor clarified. "Though you'll probably find a tunic is less difficult to wear when you change form." When Tristan raised his eyes he saw Alastor had reverted to his full demon form, complete with horns and tail. He wore an old-fashioned tunic, his standard attire when going to the Underworld.

Tristan had forgotten any demon who entered the Underworld did so in their demon form rather than their human disguise.

He'd taken his full demon form just once before, when he'd lost his temper with Lawrence the first time he'd seen him after becoming an incubus. He'd reverted back to human form after his temper had cooled and hadn't tried to change back again since.

Alastor stepped closer, his cloven hooves loud on the tiled floor. When he spoke, his voice was thicker. "Tristan, baby, whether you appear as you do now or as a true demon, you are still beautiful to me. But in the Underworld, there's no choice. You *must* take your other form before going down there."

"I don't know how to," Tristan said. "Not without losing my temper and control."

Alastor took Tristan's hands in his own. "It's okay. In this I can help you. Close your eyes and let me guide you."

Tristan squeezed the clawed fingers and waited while Alastor did what he needed to push Tristan's shields aside.

"There you are." When Tristan gathered the courage to open his eyes, Alastor smiled, his admiration obvious. "My beautiful, golden incubus."

Tristan glared down at his yellow-gold arms and clawed hands. They rested on the furred animal legs which stretched down to his set of hooves. He pulled the hooves from the now unsuitable shoes he had been wearing and sighed. "I'm not beautiful," he answered miserably. "I'm hideous."

"*Beautiful*," Alastor amended firmly. "Golden and gorgeous. I've never seen a demon like you before, and I've seen a *lot* of demons in the centuries since I died."

Mac stepped up beside them and Tristan twisted away from him. He felt awkward and uncomfortable in front of the gorgeous angel.

"Don't hide from me." Mac placed a hand on Tristan's shoulder and with the other he turned him back to face him.

"How can you even stand to look at me?"

"Because I love you," Mac focused a stern expression on Alastor. "Keep him safe."

"Of course," Alastor assured him. "Now, hold my hand, Tristan, and let me take you down to the Underworld."

"You'll stay with me?" Tristan gazed at Alastor hopefully.

"I'll have to take you down there since I suspect you don't remember the arrival chamber from our last visit. You were rather out of it at the time. I'll guide you to the Demon King's throne room, but from that point you'll be on your own."

"Do you think he'll help?" Mac interrupted. "Raphael refused, and I know he has the power to undo this."

"Raphael is a sanctimonious git," Alastor snarled, before adding in a slightly louder voice. "And I don't care if the little eavesdropper can hear me."

Tristan tugged Alastor's hand to regain his attention before things escalated into a full-blown fight. "The Underworld, please?"

Alastor wrapped Tristan up in his arms and held him close. Tristan was sure it wasn't strictly necessary to hold him so tightly, but it didn't stop him clinging on with desperation as the penthouse, Mac, and Cody disappeared and the murky caverns of the Underworld replaced them.

* * * *

The arrival chamber was nothing more than a huge cavern, dimly lit and smelling strongly of sulfur. Tristan was reminded of the old chemistry lab at his school. He'd always hated science. Many tunnels led off the chamber, none of them very inviting and some, quite terrifying. Tristan thought he saw something snake-like disappearing into one of the tunnels and he hoped they weren't going down that one. He shivered and tried to find something pleasant to focus on. Since the only thing comforting in the Underworld was Alastor, Tristan concentrated on him.

"You okay, baby?" Alastor guided Tristan through the demons congregating in the arrival chamber. Tristan could feel the stares of many of the demons on him as they entered one of the larger twisting tunnels, thankfully not the one the snake had gone down. He was glad Alastor was with him, as he suspected he'd have been wandering the Underworld for months if he'd been down there on his own.

Strange sounds and screams echoed from nearly every direction. Tristan inched closer to Alastor and cringed at every loud noise that assaulted his ears.

They arrived at the entrance to the throne room after walking the tunnels for nearly ten minutes. Alastor let go of Tristan's hand and gave him a quick kiss on the lips. "You'll have to go from here alone," he told him. "I'll be right outside if you need me. Just send your thoughts to me, and me alone, and I'll come in there. Can you do that?"

Tristan nodded. With a lot of practice over the last couple of weeks he'd finally managed to achieve the focus necessary to communicate his thoughts to a single person, and not every demon, angel, and random psychic in the immediate vicinity.

"I'll be okay," he assured Alastor before entering the throne room alone.

The Demon King was as he remembered him — large, imposing, and hideously ugly. He sat on a throne made of bones, as the demon kneeling at his feet begged for mercy.

Several other demons lingered in the room and they collectively cringed when the unlucky demon disappeared in a flash of fire.

"Next," the Demon King barked.

No one seemed to want to step forward and make their own request. Tristan's own feet seemed glued to the floor and he lingered in the doorway.

"Tristan, baby, are you okay?" Alastor's thoughts calmed him, and he breathed a little easier.

"Just scared to death," he admitted. *"How could you tell something was wrong?"*

"Two other demons just scurried out of there like rats deserting a sinking ship. Thought I'd better check on you."

"Thanks. He's not in a good mood right now."

"He rarely is. There's never a good time to ask him for anything. Just make sure to blame Lawrence for this mess and hopefully he'll take his anger out on him."

Tristan took a deep breath. None of the other demons seemed eager to draw the attention of the Demon King to themselves, so Tristan stepped forward cautiously and sank awkwardly to his knees in front of the throne.

"And what have we here?" the Demon King asked. "I don't recall seeing you before."

Tristan looked up. "I'm Tristan Garrett."

The Demon King laughed. "Only mortals need surnames. Try again."

Tristan ducked his head as several demons snickered. "I'm Tristan, incubus."

"Incubus?" The Demon King stood up and stepped forward. He reached out with a gnarled and clawed hand to lift Tristan's chin. "Well, well, well. I see you survived the change. How are you enjoying your new immortality?"

Tristan suspected the whole truth wouldn't garner him any favors, so he tried for a partial truth instead. "I'm starting a new life with Alastor and Machidiel."

The Demon King's eyes narrowed. Clearly he'd said the wrong thing.

"You're newly born, so perhaps you don't know all the rules yet, so let me tell you, never *ever* speak the name of any angel in my presence. Do so again and you will be sent straight down to the deepest pit I can find."

Tristan nodded and he clenched his hands into fists as he tried to stop shaking.

The Demon King seemed to be mollified and gestured for Tristan to continue. "And what brings you here?"

"Lawrence, the incubus who made me, froze a mortal and left me to reverse his magic. I don't have the knowledge of how to do such a thing."

"Lawrence?" The Demon King looked momentarily confused. "I thought we agreed Alastor would tutor you in our ways."

"I bargained with Lawrence for the return of my mortal memories. His price was to guide me until I found another to take my place."

"And did he return your memories?"

"He did."

"Have you chosen one to take your place with him yet?"

Tristan kept his eyes on the ground. "I find it difficult to be unfaithful to my lovers."

"Elaborate please."

Tristan wasn't sure what color his golden face turned, but he could feel the blush creeping up over his skin. When he spoke, his voice was barely more than a whisper. "I couldn't perform when I tried to feed from another."

The Demon King roared with laughter. "An impotent incubus. I've never heard of the like before."

Tristan scowled up at him. "I'm not impotent. I've been feeding from my lovers daily since the change. I just couldn't manage it with a stranger."

The Demon King collapsed back onto his throne still chuckling away. "And would you like me to help you with your performance?" he asked.

Tristan shook his head. "No. I just need to learn how to unfreeze the mortal so I can return him to his life."

"And where is he now?"

"In our flat in London."

The Demon King snapped his fingers and Cody appeared in the chamber, still frozen. He stepped closer to study him. "He isn't your usual type," he commented. "Rather scrawny, if you ask me."

Tristan bit his tongue rather than remind him he hadn't.

"This one couldn't possibly satisfy you for long."

Tristan let him criticize Cody without saying a word. As long as he helped him fix this, he didn't care what the Demon King thought of the mortal who was the latest casualty in the mess his life had become.

After an interminable length of time the Demon King waved his hand and Cody stumbled forward as the power holding him frozen dissipated.

"Welcome, mortal," the Demon King greeted him cheerfully. "Welcome to Hell."

"Am I dead?" Cody asked.

The Demon King laughed, clearly enjoying terrifying the mortal. "No, you're not dead. Do you think you've been evil enough in your life to warrant a trip down here when you do die?"

Cody cowered before the demon. "I hope not. Well, not unless I end up in Hell for being gay, like my dad says."

The Demon King smirked at Tristan. "Despite the sexual preference of your acquaintance here, being gay doesn't earn you an automatic ticket to Hell. Your father, on the other hand, should take a long hard look at his own life before it's too late. Child abusers have their own special pit down below."

"My dad's not a child abuser!"

The Demon King raised what passed for an eyebrow. "Are you telling me your father never raised a hand to you? That the night he found you on your knees, sucking another man's cock, he didn't beat you hard enough to loosen your teeth?"

"I was eighteen."

The Demon King waved away his comment. "It matters not. It isn't my place to judge whether he comes down here or not. Perhaps you're right and he's merely a thug who beats up his gay son. Maybe he can still get into Heaven. Then again, Tristan here was a good man and you can see where he ended up."

Cody stared down at Tristan who still groveled on the damp stone floor. Tristan avoided his eyes as he cringed in shame.

The Demon King sat down on his throne and grinned evilly at them. "Well, I seem to have solved the problem of the frozen mortal, so now let us discuss payment."

Tristan bit his lip. Of course he wasn't going to help him out of the goodness of his heart. Everything had a price. He hoped he could pay it. "What do you wish from me?"

Clawed fingers tapped on the bones of the throne. "I must think on this. Feel free to explore while I consider my options. But do not leave the Underworld until after I've summoned you back here."

Tristan nodded then backed toward the door, pulling Cody along with him.

Chapter Six

Alastor stood waiting right where Tristan had left him. "I see your boy's moving again," he commented and held out his hand. "We haven't been properly introduced. I'm Alastor, Tristan's partner."

Cody hesitated before taking the clawed hand and shaking it quickly. He drew back as fast as he could. "I'm Cody." He frowned as though he wasn't sure of himself. "I'm a landscape gardener, not a garden gnome."

Alastor laughed. "I meant no offense with my words. I like to make light of situations when I can. Tristan will tell you I meant no harm."

"He has a dreadful sense of humor." Tristan slid closer to Alastor, letting the older demon draw him into his embrace. "He says I can't leave until he's decided on payment. Can you take Cody back to LA and wipe his memories of all this?"

Alastor shook his head. "Only you can return him back to where you found him. LA is not just a huge place, it's one I'm not particularly familiar with. I won't risk dropping him off in the wrong neighborhood. We'll get him home as soon as we're back above ground."

"Can you take him back to the penthouse then?" Tristan asked. "Mac will be wondering where he disappeared to."

"I'm sure Mac knows exactly where he is. Besides, how do you know he doesn't want the tour of Hell?"

"Because I don't really want the tour of Hell, so I very much doubt he does."

"Maybe not, but I suspect our master back there didn't intend either of you to leave until payment has been made. So, like it or not, we're all going to be cooling our heels down here for a while yet."

"I don't mind," Cody interrupted. "Maybe it'll keep me on the straight and narrow if I know what's in store for me if I don't."

"See," Alastor said. "You're outvoted. Come on, we'll go camp out in a cave and wait for the summons."

"A cave?" Tristan asked.

"Many demons choose to live down here in the catacombs. I try not to stay here unless I have to, but I'm sure there'll be a cave we can squat in while we're waiting."

Tristan hadn't even realized some demons actually chose to live in the Underworld. He let the older demon lead them through the twisting and turning tunnels until they eventually reached a huge cavern with dozens of small entrances covering the walls. Countless ladders led to the higher caves, although some demons had wings enabling them to fly up to upper levels. "Why don't you have wings?" Tristan asked, as Alastor led them to a ladder and began to climb.

"What is it with you and your fascination with wings?" Alastor grumbled. "You might not have noticed, but you don't have a pair either."

"Just wondered." Tristan grinned. "You know I love you even without wings."

"Yeah, yeah," Alastor muttered as he swung to the side and gracefully entered one of the empty caves. "Give me your hand, baby."

Tristan reached out to take Alastor's hand and let him pull him into the cave. Cody followed close behind and soon they were all in the dark cave.

Alastor pulled a tatty, threadbare sheet across the entrance of the cave, lit a sconce on the wall, and sat down on a thin and uncomfortable-looking mattress. Tristan screwed up his nose before gingerly joining him.

"I know it's not exactly the Ritz. It's not as though I stay here unless I have to." Alastor faced Cody and shrugged. "You might as well take a seat. We could be waiting a while for the summons."

Cody sat on the floor in the far corner with his back to the wall. He kept glancing toward the entrance, as though he expected an invasion of demons at any moment.

"No one will disturb us," Alastor told him. "Just try to relax."

"Relax?" Cody laughed without humor. "I'm sitting in a cave in Hell with two demons. Relax, he says."

Tristan nudged Alastor. "Is there anything you can do to help him?"

"Such as?"

"I don't know. *Persuade* him to take it easy."

Alastor caught his meaning and focused on Cody without the mortal noticing. "Relax, Cody. We'll be out of here in no time. Just sit back and let your worries go."

As Alastor spoke, repeating his entreaty, Cody stilled. He stopped glancing at the entrance and fidgeting.

"It's like the demon version of a chill pill," Tristan murmured to Alastor.

"Far more effective than that," Alastor proudly replied.

Tristan sighed and leaned back against Alastor, using him as a cushion and wishing they were alone. "What do you think the Demon King's price will be?" he asked. "What will he want from me?"

"I don't know. It could be anything. If we're lucky, he'll just want some entertainment."

"Entertainment?"

"A floor show for him to get off to."

"I don't do public sex."

"You might have to. Or he might want something else entirely. It depends what sort of a mood he's in. Did he comment on your coloring?"

"No."

"Which means he's as intrigued by it as I am."

"What do you mean?"

"I told you, I've never seen a golden demon before, and neither has he, I'll bet. If he didn't say anything, it means he didn't want to admit you're something he hasn't seen before."

"Since arriving here, I've seen lots of different colored demons," Cody commented quietly. "What's so special about a golden one?"

Alastor smiled. "Whatever color demons you've seen, there are hundreds and thousands out there who share that color. I'm one of thousands. Tristan, however, is one-of-a kind and unique, even amongst demons."

"It makes me feel even more like a freak than I do already," Tristan muttered, as he snuggled closer to Alastor.

Alastor slapped him on his thigh. "You're not a freak. Now, try and sleep. I know you didn't get much last night."

Tristan yawned. "How did you know that?"

"Because you tossed and turned all night and I have the bruises to prove it."

Tristan closed his eyes and tried not to think about what the Demon King would want from him. As one horrifying thought after another raced through his mind, he considered that public sex was the least of his problems.

* * * *

Alastor stroked Tristan soothingly as he drifted off to sleep. As soon as Tristan was lost to slumber, his demon visage retreated and he returned to his human form. Alastor changed his own appearance as well. In the safety of the cave, they could take the risk of changing form if they wished. Alastor sighed deeply. *Could this get any more fucked up?*

He wondered whether he should be doing something to entertain Cody while he was, effectively, his guest here.

"Are you okay?" he asked eventually.

Cody nodded and drew his knees up to his chest. "Why did Tristan pick me up tonight?"

Alastor didn't have a clue on that one. He of all people knew the type Tristan usually went for. He went for strong and powerful men. Not demonic or angelic powerful, just powerful enough to keep him sated in the bedroom, or wherever else they chose to make love. He didn't think Tristan was even attracted to physically smaller men.

Of course Tristan, the incubus, had a strong desire to overpower his lovers as he fed. Alastor, like Tristan, was a switch himself, but even Mac, who far preferred to top his lovers, willingly let Tristan feed from him whenever he couldn't slake his hunger with Alastor. Was Cody Tristan's way of telling them they weren't doing enough? That *they* weren't enough?

"Alastor?" Cody prompted.

"I don't know," Alastor admitted. "You're not exactly his usual type."

"So I've seen. How long have you three been together?"

"Since last Halloween."

"And the three of you live together, like...as a couple, but with three of you?"

"That's right. It works for us."

"I guess it's not something I've really thought about. I've had enough trouble finding one guy."

"How old are you?" Alastor asked, more to make conversation than for any other reason.

"Twenty-one."

"You've plenty of time yet."

"Doesn't seem like it. I thought maybe Tristan was the one, but I guess not."

Alastor smiled down at Tristan. "He must have seen something in you he liked or he wouldn't have tried anything with you."

"He didn't like me that much," Cody mumbled. "We didn't even fuck."

Alastor didn't know what to say to reassure the young man sitting across from him, especially when a part of him rejoiced Tristan hadn't been able to follow through on his pick-up.

They sat in uncomfortable silence for several long minutes.

Alastor quietly studied the sleeping man sprawled across his lap. He suspected he and Mac should have a talk with Tristan as soon as they returned home. Alastor didn't know about Mac, but he had to be sure Tristan wanted this relationship. He just didn't know how he could bear to let him go if he wanted out.

"You love him, don't you?" Cody asked. "Even though you're demons, you love him?"

"Being evil incarnate doesn't make you incapable of feeling love." Alastor stroked Tristan's blond hair back behind his ear to stop it tickling his nose. "Though you'll find certain demons, like myself, are rather loath to admit their feelings."

"Tristan didn't seem very evil to me."

Alastor laughed. "Tristan's something of an exception to the rule, at least in my opinion."

"How so?"

"I became a demon after making a deal to buy my way out of Hell after I died. Tristan was recruited while he still lived and is one of the best men I've known. He didn't want this life and has done his best to be the same good man he was while he was mortal."

"Then not all demons are evil?"

"It depends on your point of view. Tristan would say yes, but I disagree."

"What of the other guy you live with?" Cody asked. "What was his name again?"

"Mac. He's not a demon. He's an angel, a healer."

"I gathered as much when he called Raphael—fuck, was that really the actual Raphael?"

"Unfortunately, yes." Alastor snorted with annoyance. "He could have unfrozen you if he wanted to. If it weren't for him, we wouldn't be cooling our heels down here."

"I'm sure he had his reasons."

"Probably had a wager going with one of the other archangels on how long you'd be stuck like that and he didn't want to lose."

Cody didn't seem to believe him and Alastor didn't feel like destroying all of his fantasies about the goodness of angels.

"Anyway," Cody continued. "I meant, what does Mac think about demons and whether they're evil or not?"

"Mac's current assignment is to try to save me and Tristan from our lives of evil."

"Is that why he's with you? To save you?"

"No, it's because he loves us. Though I sometimes wonder why he loves me since I've not done a great deal to earn his affection."

Cody gestured to Tristan and smiled. "Perhaps he sees how you take care of Tristan."

"Since it's my fault Tristan's a demon, I don't think I'm doing a particularly good job of looking after him."

"You made him a demon?"

"It might have been better for him if I had, but no. I'm just the one who fucked things up and ruined his life for him."

"Does he think that?"

"No, I don't," Tristan said quietly, surprising Alastor, who had thought he still slept. He sat up and turned to grasp Alastor's face in his hands. "It wasn't your fault, no more than it was Mac's fault, or even Lawrence's fault. I failed the test of temptation. Just me, no one else. I got into this mess and now I have to live with the consequences."

Alastor opened his mouth to argue, but before he could say a word, Tristan had captured his lips in a firm kiss. His tongue entered Alastor's mouth, deepening their connection.

Part of Alastor wanted to pull back and save this for their bedroom, yet another part wanted to give Cody a show. After all, once his memory was removed, he'd not recall what he'd seen anyway.

He reached down and cupped Tristan's arse, pulling him round to straddle his lap. Their clothes hadn't changed back and Alastor's thin tunic rose, thanks to his growing erection.

Tristan's own arousal pressed against him and he pulled him closer still. He could feel bare buttocks as his hands slipped beneath Tristan's tunic, tugging the fabric up to his waist.

He'd never been one for public sex. He didn't count it when it was himself, Tristan, and Mac all together. No matter who did what to whom, they all actively participated. Now there was just the two of them, with Cody watching from the other side of the cave.

Alastor wondered how far Tristan would let him go before he remembered they weren't alone.

Cody didn't seem to mind the show. There was a growing bulge in his jeans and his breath had quickened. Alastor gave the mortal a tiny nod, letting him know he could enjoy the show and take his own pleasure from watching them.

Cody unzipped his jeans and slipped his hand inside.

Alastor smiled into Tristan's mouth and turned his attention back to his lover. He swept his hand over his lover's arse again. Beneath the tunic, he dipped his fingers between Tristan's buttocks, creeping ever closer to his prize.

Tristan wriggled on his lap and ground their arousals together. He shifted his position and wrapped his legs around Alastor's back, locking him in their grip.

Alastor let his fingers wander farther still, until he found Tristan's puckered hole and pushed two of them carefully inside. Tristan groaned into his mouth and wriggled back on his fingers eagerly. *"More,"* demanded Tristan, the word a shout in Alastor's mind. He hoped it had reached Alastor alone and not the rest of the demon population in the vicinity. Although Tristan had become quite adept at focusing his telepathy, the times he was most likely to slip up were when he was in the throes of passion.

"We've no lube here, baby," Alastor reminded him.

"Don't care. Need to feel you."

"Are you sure?"

"More," Tristan repeated and Alastor slipped a third finger inside.

"Not enough. More?" Alastor knew what he wanted. Could they go so far with an audience?

"Alastor, please," Tristan begged.

Alastor couldn't resist his plea. He removed his fingers and pushed their tunics aside. He pulled away from Tristan's lips, spat into his hand, and prepared them as best he could in the circumstances. Then he tugged Tristan into position and entered him swiftly.

"Oh fuck," Tristan cried out loud. "Yes, that's it, right there. Oh god, more, Alastor, more."

"Try not to call out for god while we're down here," Alastor teased, as he pushed in a little more, highlighting to Tristan he hadn't taken him all yet.

Tristan got the point and sank down to swallow him completely.

"Okay baby?" Alastor cooed, as Tristan panted and rocked on his lap.

Tristan groaned while he tried to find the spot that always sent him soaring.

In the months they'd been together, Alastor had learned quite a lot about Tristan. He knew having his lovers play with his nipples brought Tristan to orgasm faster than nearly anything else. Alastor tweaked the nubs hard and Tristan groaned as he threw his head back. "Like that?" Alastor asked, as he brought Tristan forward and took one of the peaked buds in his mouth, sucking the nub through the fabric of his tunic.

"Oh yeah."

Alastor was close to coming and he knew he wouldn't be able to hold back much longer. Tristan continued to move up and down on his cock as Alastor sucked on his nipple. *"Tell me what you want, baby."*

"I want it hard."

"How hard?"

"Fuck me, bite me. I don't care what you do, just make me feel it."

Alastor knew that since turning into a demon, Tristan liked a little pain with his pleasure and he bit down hard on one of his nipples while he pinched the other tightly between his fingers.

"Fuck!" Tristan screamed as he came. Alastor held him as he collapsed in his arms. His own cock was still rock hard and buried in Tristan's arse.

"Love you, baby," he murmured into Tristan's mind, because some things weren't for the ears of a stranger.

Tristan smiled and sat up. *"Love you, too."* He began to rock once more, this time keeping up the gentle motion until Alastor came, buried deep inside him.

The cave smelled of sex and it wasn't just himself and Tristan. Across the room, Cody cast about for something to clean his hand with.

"There are some rags in the basket over there." Alastor pointed to the wicker basket in the back corner of the room.

Cody hurried across to grab one to clean himself up.

"Oh shit," Tristan muttered.

Alastor chuckled. "Did you forget we have company?"

"I'm such a slut," Tristan mumbled.

"A slut would have been able to fuck him earlier," Alastor pointed out. "Now, come on and clean up, baby. Cody isn't embarrassed, so you shouldn't be either."

Tristan stumbled to his feet and Alastor reached out to steady him.

"I don't do public sex," Tristan reminded him.

Alastor laughed. "You're happy to fuck either me or Mac in front of the other, it's not so different."

"It is when it's a complete stranger watching us!"

Alastor picked up one of the cleanest rags in the basket and passed it to Tristan. "Cody isn't a stranger though, is he?"

"As good as," Tristan argued, as he lifted his tunic to wipe the drying semen from his belly. "Oh yuck," he complained. "I don't think this rag has been washed in a hundred years."

"I doubt it ever has been," Alastor said.

Tristan snorted. "Remind me to educate you on the use of the washing machine when we get home."

Cody snickered and turned away while Alastor tried to hide his own smile.

"I'm perfectly capable of using a washing machine, as well you know. If you can find one in the Underworld, be sure to point me in the right direction."

Tristan continued to grumble as he tried to clean himself up without the benefit of a power shower or bathtub. Alastor rolled his eyes at Cody before turning to wipe his own cock clean.

Cody returned to his seat in the corner and Tristan and Alastor sat back on the mattress. "How long do you think we're going to have to wait?" Cody finally asked.

"Don't know," Alastor admitted. "Could be a couple of hours, or even a couple of months."

"Months?"

"Time shouldn't have moved on back in the real world. All being well, you won't have been missed when we return you."

"All being well?" Cody asked at the same time Tristan said, "Shouldn't?"

Alastor wished he'd been more careful in choosing his words.

"I thought down here worked the same as up in Heaven." Tristan twisted round to meet his lover's eyes. "We go back to the exact time we left so long as we control our return, but if a demon more powerful sends us back, we can end up anywhere from the time we left onwards?"

"Mostly it works like that," Alastor confirmed. "But what you have to remember is down here there are places where time gets a bit screwed up."

"What do you mean?"

"Imagine suffering through the worst moment of your life for the rest of eternity. Or experiencing the pain of your death over and over again. To inflict that sort of torture on someone requires time to be replayed or stretched out and slowed down. If you wander too far into the bowels of Hell, you could find years have passed down here and seconds up on Earth, or maybe it's the other way round with a second here, while the real world has moved on a century or more."

"Shit!"

Alastor gave his two guests a grim smile. "Don't worry. We shouldn't be going down far enough to get caught up in any sort of time distortion. We'll be home again either the exact moment we left or after however much time has passed for us here, depending on who controls our return."

"But we could still be waiting round here for months?" Cody looked like he'd rather be anywhere else and Alastor didn't blame him in the slightest. It wasn't exactly home sweet home in the cave.

"It probably won't be as long as all that," Alastor tried to assure him. "He takes longer to summon people when you want something from him. When it's him calling you to give him something he wants, he tends to be quicker."

"I'm still undecided as to whether that's a good thing or a bad," Tristan muttered.

"Can I ask something?" Cody asked.

"If you like," Alastor replied.

"Does it hurt when you change from a human to — you know — the demon?"

"No." Alastor switched back to his demon form to demonstrate. "This is what I am. The human form is simply what I choose when I'm out in public up there."

"I thought the human form was the real one," Tristan said. "I thought that was why I kept going back to that one and why I couldn't change into a demon except when I lost my temper."

"I'm afraid not. The demon form is your true form now."

"Then why can I keep the human form without trying and struggle to take demon form?"

"Because you haven't accepted your demon side yet," Alastor explained. "When you're comfortable with this side of you, you'll be able to switch from one form to the other as easily as I do. At the moment, you're still rejecting your demon side and you're building shields against it."

Alastor nudged at the shields until Tristan's form changed once again.

"I don't think I'll ever be comfortable with being a demon." Tristan picked at the fur on his thighs and Alastor took hold of his hand to stop him from making a bald patch on his leg.

"Stop picking at your fur," he scolded affectionately.

Tristan sighed. "Do you have any idea how wrong that sounds?"

"Then don't pick at it," Alastor teased. "Now, how about we think of some way to pass the time while we're waiting?"

"A way that doesn't involve sex," Tristan amended, with a pointed look at the others. "I can't believe we just shagged in front of a stranger. What the fuck was I thinking?"

"You were thinking you were horny and didn't care whether we had an audience at the time."

Tristan shot Alastor a glare. "Can you at least try to be embarrassed about it?"

"I'm not going to pretend to be embarrassed," Alastor told him. "You needed to get off, so did I, and so did Cody. We're all better off now the tension has been released, so what's the problem?"

"Let's not argue," Cody interrupted. "Why don't you tell me how you met or something?"

"In a nightclub," Alastor began and they passed the next couple of hours talking about their meeting and the events that had followed, leading right up to the night Tristan had gone with Lawrence to find a human to fuck.

Cody listened intently as Alastor talked.

"And so this demon, Lawrence, he's still bound to Tristan, right?"

Tristan answered his question. "Unfortunately. Though maybe with a bit of luck, we'll still be stuck here when he turns up for my next lesson."

Alastor doubted whether Tristan's absence would deter Lawrence for long. They needed to find a way to remove him from their lives for good, but in a way Tristan could live with.

He studied Cody as they waited for the summons. The mortal seemed to be taking things rather well, considering. Perhaps he might be amenable to the idea of immortality. Although Alastor didn't relish the idea of turning Cody into a killer and leaving him in the clutches of Lawrence, he liked the idea of Tristan stuck with him even less.

Fuck. What am I thinking? He was seriously considering persuading Tristan to turn Cody. He could do it too. His best and most powerful demonic power was the ability to bend others to his will. All he had to do was give Tristan a push in the right direction and voila. Like Tristan said, Cody was just a stranger. Mac wouldn't approve, but if it broke Tristan's bargain with Lawrence, surely he'd not interfere?

Chapter Seven

Tristan heard the summons in his mind as clearly as if the Demon King stood in front of him. He wasn't sure how long they had been waiting around — certainly it had been long enough for Cody to nod off to sleep in the corner.

Tristan pulled out of Alastor's arms and called across to the mortal. "Hey, Cody, we're being summoned back."

Cody opened his eyes and jumped back startled, as though he'd forgotten where he was. With a little demonic intervention from Alastor he recovered quickly and sat up. "What time is it?" he asked.

"No idea," Tristan admitted. "We'd better hurry. Even though time doesn't move the same down here, I suspect he won't want to be kept waiting. He wants both of us there."

Alastor had already climbed out of the cave and it wasn't long before they arrived back at the Throne Room.

"Remember," he murmured into Tristan's ear as he nuzzled his neck. "No matter the price he asks, you'll have to pay it — no questions, no arguments."

Tristan nodded once and together with Cody, he walked into the Throne Room again.

The Demon King lounged on the throne of bones. The other lingering demons had all departed. One other demon was in the room besides the three of them and Lawrence didn't appear happy to be there.

Tristan dropped to his knees besides Lawrence. Cody stood at his other side, but he didn't bow to the king. Tristan wondered if the Demon King would take issue about the lack of respect, but he let the slight pass without a comment.

"Thank you for returning to see me," the Demon King said, as though they had any choice in the matter. "As you can see, I've summoned Lawrence before me to deal with the issue of the willful exposure of our kind to a mortal."

Tristan glanced at Lawrence and saw his thin lips press together in annoyance. *Good,* He hoped his punishment was swift in coming and designed to keep him away from Tristan for the foreseeable future.

"My king," Lawrence began. "I merely sought to ensure Tristan used his powers to the best of his ability."

The Demon King stood and stalked toward the three of them. He loomed over Lawrence and glared down at him. "Did you tell the mortal about our kind and leave a new demon to wipe his memory?"

"Tristan has the help of Alastor and the angel to wipe his memory," Lawrence pointed out.

"And if Alastor was busy doing something for me at the time?" The Demon King suggested it as though this had been the case and not merely an afterthought.

"Then the angel would have been there."

"It isn't the job of the angels to clean up *your* mess. You left a human frozen and with the knowledge of our kind."

"Tristan has the power to unfreeze him."

"Tristan is a new demon and barely in control of his hunger. Only the fact his lovers are immortal keeps him from taking a life every time he feeds. You expect him to have mastered within weeks the same powers you took decades to wield?"

Lawrence continued to bow his head as the Demon King's voice grew in volume, echoing throughout the cavern.

The Demon King leaned down and growled. "Then there's your attempt to undermine my authority by entering into your bargain with Tristan in the first place."

"No, my king," Lawrence stammered. "He wanted the return of his memories and we made the bargain in good faith."

"I chose Alastor to teach Tristan our ways. You bargained to take over his duty in direct contravention of my decision."

"I didn't mean to." Lawrence cast around the room, as though someone might suddenly appear and speak up for him.

The Demon King towered over the cowering demon. "A few centuries in the pit should be sufficient to remind you of your place."

"No." Lawrence turned to Tristan. "Tristan, tell him you agreed to our bargain. Tell him you wanted me to train you. Tell him he can't do this."

Tristan shook his head and shuffled away from Lawrence. "He knows I made the bargain, and he knows why."

"Correct," the Demon King agreed. "I am also well aware Tristan didn't have his memories when he made the bargain with you, and thus had no way of knowing his bargain would be against my wishes."

Tristan ducked his head to hide the fact he knew that wasn't strictly true. Alastor had told him of the events in the Underworld and the decision the Demon King had made regarding his training not long after he'd turned.

It seemed Lawrence's luck had run out and the Demon King's patience was at an end. Flames sprang from the cracks in the floor, surrounded Lawrence, and sucked him down with them as they receded.

"Your bargain with Lawrence is broken," the Demon King announced.

"And my memories?" Tristan asked. "What happens to those?"

The Demon King waved away his question. "Keep them — they hold no interest for me. Now, about my payment."

Tristan nodded and waited patiently.

"This mortal — who seems to have been in the center of the most recent troubles — he is my payment."

Tristan's eyes widened as he faced the Demon King who strolled back to his throne.

"No." Cody's voice was barely more than a whisper. Tristan wasn't sure whether the Demon King was ignoring him or whether he simply hadn't heard him. "Tristan, please. You said I'd be returned home."

Tristan squeezed his eyes closed and sent his thoughts to Alastor. *"His price is Cody."*

"Fuck."

"What should I do?"

Alastor's sigh drifted into his mind. *"I'm sorry, baby. You have no choice."*

Tristan opened his eyes and faced the Demon King. "Agreed," he whispered, as though he'd ever had a choice.

"Tristan, *no.*" Cody grabbed hold of his arm tight. "You can't leave me down here. You have to take me home."

"I'm sorry," Tristan offered — and he truly was.

"Tristan, please." Tears welled up in Cody's eyes as he pleaded. He was twenty one and hadn't done anything wrong except get picked up by a demon. Now he had been consigned to a future in Hell.

The Demon King let Cody plead for a few more minutes. Tristan suspected he actually enjoyed their misery, maybe even feeding on it the same way Tristan fed from sex.

Finally, he seemed to come to the conclusion that enough was enough and he waved a hand toward Cody, causing a chain to snake across the floor and the manacle on the end to clasp around his ankle. The chain glowed for a moment before vanishing.

"It may be invisible, but it's still there," the Demon King explained. "You will have free run of the Underworld, but if you try to leave, the chain will prevent you. Now, your attire is unsuitable." He paused and contemplated Cody for a moment. Then Tristan watched as Cody's clothes vanished and he stood naked before them.

"Please," Cody begged, this time to the Demon King, as he covered himself as best he could with his hands.

"I wish to view all of you," the Demon King stated. "You will be clothed suitably as soon as I've looked you over."

Cody shifted uncomfortably and the blush on his face extended down his neck until it seemed to Tristan as though his whole body was flushed.

"I must admit," the Demon King commented. "I'm struggling to find the flaw that stopped the incubus from feeding upon you. What prevented you from fucking him, Tristan?"

Tristan bowed his head. "I don't know. I just couldn't go through with it."

"Because of your feelings for Alastor and the angel?"

"I think so."

The Demon King ran a clawed finger down Cody's chest. "I wonder if Alastor would have been so reluctant to take him. He has had many lovers over the centuries you know."

Tristan had suspected as much from various comments Alastor had made. His lover's history didn't make any difference to how Tristan felt about him. He knew his lover remained faithful to him and Mac these days.

"Perhaps I should call him in to join us," the Demon King suggested with a glance toward the entrance. "He lingers just outside the chamber after all."

Tristan remained silent and the Demon King turned back to Cody, fingering his hair and caressing his face with his clawed hand.

Cody's eyes held Tristan's own, silently pleading with him to make this right, to get him out of there. Tristan wanted to look away, close his eyes, anything to avoid seeing the silent recrimination in the tearful brown eyes of the mortal.

"Leave us," the Demon King ordered, and Tristan fled from the room as fast as he could.

"Tristan?" Cody's soft cry followed him.

Tristan threw himself into Alastor's arms with a sob of his own.

"Not here," Alastor said. "Never show weakness in the Underworld. Hold it together for just a moment longer, baby."

Tristan drew in a deep breath, and Alastor transported them back to the penthouse.

* * * *

Mac had watched Alastor and Tristan vanish to the Underworld and Cody disappear from under his gaze a moment later. When Alastor and Tristan returned alone, he knew something was wrong.

Hurrying to his lovers, he took Tristan in his arms and held him as he fell apart. "It's okay, love. It's okay."

Tristan pushed out of Mac's arms and glared at him. "It's not fucking okay. Cody's still down there and we've no way of releasing him. Why the fuck didn't Raphael unfreeze him when you asked him to? If he'd just done that one little thing, he'd be home now instead of trapped in the Underworld."

Mac didn't blame Tristan for being angry with the archangel—he was far from pleased with Raphael himself. Anger and shouting wasn't going to fix things though. "Alastor, what happened?"

Alastor sat down in the corner of the sofa and told Mac what had transpired in the Underworld. "At least the bargain with Lawrence is broken," he concluded. It was the one good thing to come out of the journey into the Underworld.

"Will he grow bored with Cody perhaps?" Mac asked, after Alastor had finished recounting the events. "Let him leave and return to his life after he's done with his new pet?"

Alastor shrugged. "I don't know. Human pets in the Underworld aren't a new thing, though this particular king has never had one before now. He may keep him for just a short time, but even a few weeks could damage Cody irreparably."

"Won't he erase his mind when he sends him home?" Tristan asked.

"He doesn't have to, if he doesn't want to," Alastor explained. "Cody wouldn't be believed if he tried to tell anyone what had happened to him and he'd merely be viewed as a crazy, young man, his future in ruins."

"But won't that expose demons to the world, just the same as he punished Lawrence for?" Tristan asked. "It seems rather hypocritical to send Lawrence down to be tortured, while doing the same thing himself."

"No one ever said demons were consistent." Alastor brushed some dirt from his tunic and sighed. "Now, I don't know about you, but I'm filthy and tired. I'm going to take a shower and crash for a few hours. You should probably clean up too."

Tristan agreed and Mac watched the two of them leave for the bathroom.

Mac was worried about Cody, yet not as worried as he was for Tristan. The young human he'd fallen in love with had been put through so much in the last few weeks and Mac wasn't sure how much more he could take. Sooner or later he would reach his limit and Mac had no idea how he would cope when he did.

In the meantime Mac wanted answers from Raphael as to why he had stood by and let an innocent man suffer when he had the power to prevent it.

* * * *

The Realm of Angels appeared tranquil and peaceful when Mac arrived in search of the archangel. It was a direct contrast to how he felt right now. He found Raphael guiding human souls who had chosen to be reincarnated into a new life through the archway leading back to Earth. Mac wondered sometimes whether it might have been better to be reborn instead of returning to Alastor and Tristan. He'd been charged with saving the two demons, yet he still had no idea how to go about such a task. They lived good lives, as best they could, and Mac didn't see how they could do anything more. He felt as though he'd been given an impossible task and the archangels—Raphael in particular—merely waited for him to fail.

"Machidiel." Raphael greeted him with slightly more warmth than he had shown during their last encounter.

Mac waited for Raphael to finish escorting the human on his arm before stepping aside, letting the archangel follow after him.

"Why didn't you help Cody?" Machidiel asked. "Did you know what would happen to him?"

Raphael confirmed he did. "His fate was sealed the moment he and Tristan met. Nothing could have prevented this."

"*You* could have prevented this," Mac shouted, drawing the attention of human souls and angels alike to their discussion.

"It isn't my place to interfere. If it's meant to be, then Cody will find a way out of the Underworld. I doubt he's destined to spend eternity down there, though he appears to have settled in nicely in recent weeks."

"Weeks? How long has it been for Cody?"

"A few months." Raphael didn't sound concerned.

"He's been there for months?" Mac knew how time worked in the Underworld, but this was even worse than he had thought.

"From his point of view, yes."

Mac's frustration rose with every word to fall from Raphael's lips. "We have to get him out of there before irreparable damage is done to him."

"How do you know it isn't already too late?"

Mac wouldn't accept that. "Damage to the mind can be undone by removing his memories before he's returned home."

"How do you know he wants to forget? Perhaps he'd rather remember what transpired down there. In the meantime, perhaps you've forgotten your assignment."

"I've not forgotten it. How could I?" His assignment played on his mind every day as he struggled to find a way to rescue his demon lovers.

Raphael's expression was cool. "Your assignment is to save Alastor and Tristan. Yet under your watch, Tristan made a deal with another demon and set out with the intention of preying on humans to satisfy his sexual appetite. Cody's predicament is a direct consequence of your failure."

Mac jumped back as though he'd been slapped. Much as he hated to admit it, Raphael had a point. If he'd been more careful, Lawrence would never have been alone with Tristan and none of this would have happened.

"You should return to Earth," Raphael advised. "Tristan needs you."

"What do you mean?" Mac asked, but Raphael ignored him and returned to the archway of reincarnation.

Mac didn't dare linger any longer. He returned to the penthouse, unsure what he would find on his return. He was surprised to find the place quiet. After what Raphael had told him, Mac found this most suspicious.

He wandered into the bedroom and found Alastor and Tristan, both back in their human forms, snuggling together in their new bed. Both looked to be sound asleep, though Tristan's dreams appeared to be troubled, at least if the frown on his face was anything to go by.

Mac stripped off his clothes and slid into bed with his lovers. He wrapped his arms around Tristan and held him close, whispering soothing nonsense words into his ear.

Chapter Eight

"Duach?"

Tristan turned over in his sleep and reached out for the warm body next to him.

"Duach?"

Stirring slightly, he woke just enough to realize the voice wasn't coming from whoever slept beside him. A poke in the shoulder confirmed his suspicions.

"Duach, wake up."

Tristan opened his eyes and peered into the darkness. "What time is it?" he mumbled.

"It'll be a while before dawn. Come with me."

Tristan recognized the voice, even though he couldn't see the face. He frowned at the unfamiliar words. He could tell they weren't spoken in English, yet he understood them easily. "Mac?"

"Duach, quickly, before everyone wakes."

Ignoring the strangeness of suddenly knowing another language, Tristan stumbled to his feet and followed Mac out of what appeared to be a hut. He struggled to navigate his way across the uneven floor in the dark. He grabbed Mac's hand, trusting him to see them safely through.

Outside, the world was cloaked in darkness. Tristan gazed up at the night sky and wondered at the vast array of stars. He couldn't remember ever seeing such a sight. "It's beautiful," he breathed.

Mac pulled him round the back of the hut and deep into the trees. "You're beautiful, Duach."

Tristan wondered why Mac continued to call him the strange sounding name. Things turned to a more familiar ground when Mac pushed him up against the tree and rubbed up against him passionately. Tristan groaned and pulled Mac toward him, kissing him deeply.

Mac didn't seem to realize what Tristan intended at first, but soon he began to tentatively kiss him back. Tristan placed his hands on Mac's arse and encouraged him to continue grinding against him. Tristan's heart pounded and all his blood rushed south. Mac pulled out of the kiss, gasping, his breath coming in sharp pants.

"What was that?" he asked in astonishment. Tristan had the strangest feeling Mac had no idea what a kiss was.

"Didn't you like it?" Tristan teased and he reached down to place his hand over the bulge in Mac's tunic that told him he'd enjoyed the kiss a great deal.

Mac didn't miss a beat. He reached down and rubbed Tristan through the thick fabric of his clothes in turn.

"Come away with me," Mac said. "Just the two of us."

"Of course." Tristan would follow Mac anywhere if he asked him to.

Mac tore at his clothes and Tristan did likewise. Somewhere in the back of his mind, Tristan knew he was dreaming. The world around him appeared strange and unfamiliar, the one stable point being Mac, and he clung to him.

When Mac entered him swiftly Tristan cringed at the initial pain. Why couldn't he have dreamed of Mac taking him in a five-star hotel with all the modern conveniences, including lube? No, his dream placed him somewhere in the woods, reminding him of his dreadful camping trip with Lawrence and all that had transpired since that fateful night.

Mac buried his cock deep inside him and with each thrust of Mac's hips Tristan could feel the rough bark of the tree scraping down his back. Pillows and a soft mattress were a distant memory.

Still, even the discomfort of their surroundings couldn't obliterate the pleasure that Tristan got from the feeling of being so completely filled by his lover. He clenched around Mac's dick, letting his lover use him as hard as he wanted.

Mac groaned as they moved together. Tristan's cock, aching for attention, rose between them. Tristan wanted to reach down and take himself in hand, but he needed both hands to hold himself in place.

"Oh fuck," he shouted as Mac hit his sweet spot again and again. He closed his eyes as he started to come. He felt the warmth of Mac's release filling his arse as his lover's shout of pleasure echoed through his ears. His own orgasm followed and his seed coated each of their bellies and chests.

The scream echoed through the night, causing the two of them to freeze.

Tristan stared over Mac's shoulder and saw the young woman standing on the path between the trees.

Tristan scrambled for a name, but unlike other dreams, where people he knew in real life were wont to pop up in the oddest of places, the slim, brown-haired woman was a stranger to him.

Before either he or Mac could say a word, she had turned to run back in the direction of the huts.

Mac pulled out of Tristan and hurriedly gathered his clothes.

"Mac, what's wrong?" Tristan reached out to pat Mac's shoulder. "Don't worry about her. What do we care if she got an eyeful?"

Mac glanced up from where he had stooped down to pick up Tristan's clothes. "She's your wife, and her father is leader of the clan. You know what this means?"

Tristan shook his head, stunned over the very idea of having a wife. He let Mac dress him and pull him back toward the hut. "Mac, why don't we just leave?"

Mac turned raised eyebrows toward him. "Why do you keep calling me Mac?"

"It's your name, isn't it?"

"My name's Leith, as well you know," Mac replied.

Tristan shrugged. It didn't matter what Mac chose to call himself, Tristan knew who Mac was, just as he knew who he was, despite Mac repeatedly calling him Duach.

Mac tugged on Tristan's hand. "We must hurry."

"Why? What's the worst that could happen?"

"We'll be killed," Mac told him, as though the answer were obvious. "At best, we'll merely be driven out of the village. We have to run. It's what we've always talked of. Just you and me. We'll find somewhere to settle where no one knows us or cares whether we lie together."

It sounded like a good idea to Tristan and he hurried to keep up with Mac's fast pace.

Unfortunately, they weren't quick enough and the villagers, apparently woken by Tristan's wife, awaited them when they stepped into the circle of huts.

"Duach, Leith." The man in the center of the crowd greeted them coldly. The dawn was fast approaching and in the dim early morning light Tristan realized he knew the man.

"Hi, Dad. You never met Mac, did you?"

The doppelganger of the man he had known all his life continued to glare at him. Tristan's father hadn't exactly been thrilled to find out his son was gay, but he'd always been too polite to say much on the subject. The hatred in his dad's double's eyes made Tristan shiver. He doubted this man would ever hesitate to give his opinion.

"Duach," Mac whispered. "Be careful what you say. This man is not your friend. He opposed your marriage to his daughter and would do you much harm."

Tristan couldn't imagine his father ever raising a hand to him. It didn't matter that in this dream his father was his father-in-law, his mind couldn't reconcile to the fact he might be in some form of danger.

"Is it true?" the man asked.

"You doubt my word?" his daughter interrupted, pushing her way to the front of the crowd. "I saw them with my own eyes. Rutting against each other like animals, they were."

Tristan had to shout to be heard amongst the uproar the words caused amongst the villagers. "It wasn't like that. Mac, I mean Leith, and I love each other."

Mac drew in a sharp breath just as the villagers surged toward them. Tristan struggled against the hands grabbing at him, dragging him away from Mac, from the man he knew would keep him safe.

Before he could even truly register what had happened, Tristan found himself tied with rough cords against a tree. The first strike to his back came as such a shock that bile rose in his throat and he willed himself not to vomit.

The second assault burned even more than the first. Tristan heard a cry from Mac. His lover's pain hurt almost as much as the blows to his back.

"Stop! It was me. It was all me. I seduced him. Duach didn't wish to lie with me until I suggested it."

The third strike would have sent Tristan to his knees had he not been tied up. As a demon, he wasn't entirely averse to a little pain in the bedroom, but what he experienced with his lovers was a far cry from being beaten like this.

"Please stop!" Tristan could hear the increasing desperation in Mac's voice.

"Your turn will come," one of the other villagers called out, causing a ripple of laughter throughout the audience.

Tristan closed his eyes and tried to block out the pain, but only when he slipped into unconsciousness did it finally ebb.

Tristan woke in a cold sweat, trapped between his two lovers. His stomach rolled and he clambered over Alastor to lean over the side of the bed and retch into the waste basket.

"Tristan?" Alastor appeared beside him in an instant, holding him and comforting him as he brought up the contents of his stomach. "Are you okay?"

When there was nothing left for him to bring up, Tristan collapsed onto his back and gave Alastor a droll look. "Do I look okay?"

"Dumb question, huh?" Alastor climbed off the bed and took the waste basket into the bathroom. "Can I get you anything? Water?"

"Water's good."

"I'll get it," Mac offered, returning with a glass of cold water a moment later.

Tristan sipped at the water as Alastor and Mac fussed over him. Tristan curled up against his lovers, trying to shake off the unsettling dream.

"How are you feeling now?" Alastor asked, as he brushed Tristan's hair back from his forehead.

"Okay. Just a bad dream. Probably something I ate."

"Did you eat in the Underworld?" Mac asked.

"No," Alastor answered for them both. "It's best not to sample the food down there, not if you want to risk being trapped there forever if you eat the wrong thing. I hadn't eaten since breakfast yesterday."

"Me neither," Tristan agreed. "Unless you count the alcohol at the bar in LA."

Mac grinned. "Perhaps you should stick to good old English beer from now on."

"Fine with me," Tristan chuckled. "One trip to LA was more than enough."

"A second trip will be inevitable though," Mac reminded him. "To return Cody home, remember?"

Tristan frowned. He'd almost forgotten about the mortal he had left behind in Hell. He wondered whether he should be worried about how quickly he'd pushed Cody's plight from his mind. Was it some sort of sign of his loss of humanity? "You're right. I think we should concentrate on rescuing Cody from the Underworld and returning him home."

"Come on, let's get you something light for breakfast, and we'll try to come up with a plan."

Tristan trailed into the kitchen after Mac. Alastor followed close behind and the two of them sat at the table while Mac rummaged round the fridge.

Once they were all sat at the table eating—or in Tristan's case, picking at—their breakfast, Mac raised the problem again.

"Any ideas?" Mac asked Alastor, who amongst the three of them was the authority on matters of the Underworld.

"I would have thought he'd have become bored of having a human pet fairly quickly," Alastor said. "I don't know why he hasn't returned him home."

"Raphael told me it had been several months for Cody already."

"Did he explain why he didn't step in to stop this?"

"No. You know the archangels don't explain themselves unless they have to."

"I suppose that means they don't intend to help us get Cody back."

"No, we're on our own. We have to help him or we run the risk of his life being ruined by the memories of what he's suffered down there."

"What do you mean?" Tristan asked.

"If we return him to his life, either Alastor or I can remove his memories of his time in the Underworld and replace them with something more pleasant. If he's returned home by other means, his life could potentially be ruined. We have to find a way to rescue him—and quickly."

"Do you have a plan?" Alastor asked.

Mac sighed. "I wish I did."

Tristan threw his mug of coffee across the room, smashing the china against the wall. It didn't help, but Tristan needed an outlet for his anger, and violence against inanimate objects was all he had right now. "There must be a way to help him."

"Not for us." Alastor ran his hands through his hair and Tristan saw his horns begin to sprout from his skull. He'd never seen Alastor so frustrated he couldn't stop his demon form from bleeding through to the surface.

"For someone then?" Tristan pressed. His own temper still simmered and even as he spoke his nails grew out to become claws.

"A coup," Alastor snapped, his horns now fully grown and his teeth pointed. "And we don't have that sort of power, not by a long shot. My own master didn't have the sort of power to take over the Underworld and he bloody tried."

Mac twisted round in his seat and studied Tristan. "You need to feed," he stated.

Tristan closed his eyes and took a steadying breath. Alastor's words had angered him and he wasn't sure he could stop himself from hurting him if he took the other demon right now. He turned to Mac and gestured toward the bedroom.

He cringed when he caught Alastor's expression of surprised hurt. He had been feeding mostly from Alastor since getting his memories back, since he knew Mac preferred to top while Alastor, like himself, was far more flexible when it came to who fucked who. Only when Alastor wasn't around or when feeding from the other demon wasn't quite enough to slake his appetite, did he turn to take Mac as well. For the first time he had chosen to feed from Mac first when Alastor sat right there in front of him.

Alastor watched Tristan follow Mac into the bedroom with an eerie sense of déjà vu. Tristan and Mac together and him watching from the sidelines. Damn it, what was wrong with him? He thought he'd overcome his jealousy issues long before now. Why did the green-eyed monster residing within him insist on rearing its ugly head yet again?

He had to stop this before he went stark raving mad.

Leaving the table and the dirty dishes, he walked into the bedroom to join his lovers.

Mac lay on his back, his legs hooked up over Tristan's shoulders. He saw Alastor enter and waved him over to join them.

Alastor didn't waste any time in climbing onto the bed. He pulled Mac's head to the side and kissed him hard. *"Love you,"* he whispered into Mac's mind. He'd waited so long to say the words that he made sure he spoke them whenever he felt them now. He didn't want either of his lovers to ever doubt his feelings.

Tristan's hand brushed his arm and Alastor pulled back from Mac long enough to face him. *"You're next,"* Tristan told him. *"I'm hungry this morning."*

Alastor wanted to ask why he hadn't taken him first. His nervousness over what the answer might be stopped him voicing the question. At least Tristan still wanted him, and he was happy to give his lover what he needed.

He'd do absolutely anything for his men as long as it meant he kept them in his life.

* * * *

"Sorry," Tristan offered, as they cuddled on the bed after they were all sated.

"What for?" Alastor asked, even though he suspected what Tristan might be talking about.

"For feeding from Mac first," Tristan confirmed. "I'm angry at this whole mess and I didn't want to hurt you."

Alastor laughed. "You're forgetting that of the two of us, I'm the one who gets off on a little pain." He grinned across at Mac, who appeared to be asleep. "Mac's the one who's a wuss."

Mac smacked Alastor across the chest. "Watch who you're calling a wuss," he warned, though the sleepy chuckle took the edge off his words.

"I'm not the one who waited for centuries before giving up my arse to another bloke," Alastor teased back.

Mac opened his eyes and smiled. "I gave it to you because I love you."

The strange fluttering in his chest made Alastor look away and his response was gruffly spoken. "I'm glad you waited for me."

Tristan pulled out of Alastor's embrace and stretched his arms above his head. "Much as I'd love to stay in bed all day and listen to you two cooing at each other, we still have the problem of Cody to try and sort out."

"I don't coo," Alastor muttered, as he tugged Tristan back into his arms. "And we can think in bed just as well as out of it."

Tristan snorted with amusement. "That's highly debatable. So, do you want to prove me wrong by telling me what orgasmic inspiration hit you while my cock was up your arse?"

Alastor wished he could. Unfortunately he was still at a loss as to how to put Cody back where he belonged.

"We'll find a way," Mac promised. "Everything will be okay."

"Will it?" Tristan snapped. "Just we seem to say that quite a lot and it never is. Look at me for the proof."

Mac sat up and gestured for the others to do the same. He waited until they had all risen, with none of them touching, before he spoke again. "Okay, let's try to sort things out. Tristan, would you like to go first and get whatever you need to say off your chest?"

Tristan shrugged and studied the duvet cover.

"Alastor?" Mac prompted when several minutes had passed without Tristan saying anything.

"What do you want me to say?" Alastor asked impatiently.

Mac glared across the bed at him and Alastor shifted in his spot. "How about I start then?"

Alastor waved for him to continue while Tristan nodded.

"Things haven't exactly gone as we thought when I suggested we start this relationship," Mac began. "If I'd known what would happen, I would never have taken either of you to my bed. I'm sorry."

Alastor reached out to take Mac's hand. "I'm not."

"Me neither," Tristan agreed.

Mac snorted. "Liar. If it weren't for me, you'd still be human."

"I'd be dead," Tristan corrected, as he took Mac's other hand. "You said yourself, when it's your time to die, there's no way to avoid it. My days were numbered whether I'd met you or not. Lawrence was in my life long before you two. If I hadn't met you and Alastor, I'd either be dead or an incubus like him, preying on mortals daily, and with a far higher body count to my name."

Alastor pulled Mac's hand up to his mouth and turned it so he could kiss the palm. "I have no regrets. I want the two of you so badly I can hardly bear to be apart from you."

Mac leaned forward to kiss Alastor on the lips. "We both know your issues have nothing to do with regrets and everything to do with jealousy."

Alastor ducked his head. "I don't mean to be. I just can't seem to help myself."

Tristan rubbed Alastor's arm soothingly. "You have no reason to be jealous. I love you, and if I ever had to choose between the two of you, it would be you."

Alastor frowned. "Because I'm a demon like you."

"No," Tristan said. "Because you're you."

"Really?"

Tristan slid closer and wrapped his arms around his lover. "On the night Lawrence tempted me, he asked which of you I'd choose if I had to. I'll tell you what I told him. You, Alastor."

Mac chuckled. "Perhaps I should be the jealous one?"

Tristan smiled at Mac for a moment before his face shuttered closed. "Oh." He pulled away from Alastor and his face flushed a delightful shade of pink. "I'm so stupid. It's not me, is it? It's my relationship with Mac you're jealous of. You've been in love with him for centuries then I come along and— Fuck, how could I have been so arrogant?"

Alastor watched as Tristan scrambled off the bed and bolted for the bathroom. "Oh shit!"

Before he could move to follow Tristan, Mac stopped him with a firm grip on his arm. "Alastor, wait."

Alastor turned back, not so much because of the way Mac held him, but because of the tone of his voice. "Don't say it, Mac."

Mac loosened his grasp a little. "It needs saying. I love you and I love Tristan. But do not *ever* make me choose between you."

"Because you'd choose him, wouldn't you?" Alastor knew it was the truth without Mac saying the words.

"I'm not going to answer that," Mac replied stonily. "Now I'm going to go back up there and see if I can find some help for Cody."

"I thought they wouldn't help us?"

"Raphael refused—that doesn't mean I can't ask around, maybe call in a few favors. I suggest you try to smooth things over with Tristan before I return."

Mac disappeared from the bed and Alastor followed after Tristan. He wasn't surprised to find the bathroom door locked.

He knocked on the wood. "Tristan, can I come in?"

Silence greeted his request. He wondered if he should just teleport himself to the other side of the barrier, but he stubbornly wanted Tristan to open up for him.

"Tristan, you know I love you—we both do." He knocked harder. "Damn it, Tristan, you can't hide in there all day."

No sound came from inside and Alastor chewed on his lip as he considered his options. He remembered the Halloween night he'd gone to Tristan's house, only to find the skittish young man reluctant to admit him. He'd used his powers of persuasion to give him a nudge. Would it work again now? There was one way to find out. *"Open the door, Tristan. Let me inside. Don't shut me out. Let me in. Let me in. Let me in."*

The door opened slowly and Tristan glared at him from the other side. "Maybe no one's told you that trying to force other demons into doing what you want doesn't work. Better yet, we can tell exactly what you're doing when you try to mess with our minds."

Alastor jumped back in surprise. He'd used his powers on other demons before, many times, in fact. Only those more powerful than him could tell when he'd manipulated them, and of those, barely a handful could resist his persuasion. If Tristan was immune to his greatest power, there had to be more to this than met the eye. It took just a second to decide not to correct Tristan on his assumption. "Sorry?"

Tristan rolled his eyes and turned to sit on the edge of the bathtub. "I'm sorry too. I never meant to come between the two of you."

"What? No, Tristan, you haven't." Alastor rushed to his side and knelt on the mat at Tristan's feet. "We love you. You haven't come between us at all—if anything, you've brought us together."

"And now I'm in the way."

"No." Alastor reached up to tilt Tristan's face toward his own, not an easy task since the stubborn young incubus did his utmost to avoid his gaze. "I'm a jealous idiot and I've no right to be."

Tristan finally gave him a weak smile. "Me, too, though I suspect you already know."

Alastor grinned up at him. "I do wonder why Mac puts up with either of us sometimes."

Tristan reached out and fell into Alastor's waiting arms. "He probably just goes up there to get away from us and our issues."

Alastor chuckled in amused agreement as he pulled Tristan onto his lap. "Yeah, I can always tell when he's being summoned up there and when he's avoiding me or pissed off. When he's summoned, he returns at the same moment—other times he makes me cool my heels waiting."

"Guess I must have *really* pissed him off when I killed him then."

Alastor slapped Tristan's arse. "You know that's not true. He was sent back to the time the archangels determined, and they didn't care we were missing him like crazy."

Tristan wriggled on his lap and their cocks brushed together, trapped between them. Alastor reached down to take them both in hand at the same time Tristan did likewise. Together they wrapped their hands around their aching erections and kissed as they stroked themselves and each other to completion.

Chapter Nine

It didn't take long for Mac to track down Metatron. Of all the angels, the archangels were the easiest to locate. They rarely went down to Earth these days and never for any prolonged period of time.

Metatron didn't ask questions and didn't seem to think it unusual for Mac to ask him where to find one of his charges. He merely nodded silently and sent Mac directly to Pel, who was currently on assignment in Australia.

Mac found himself standing in the middle of a busy street, with Pel walking directly toward him.

"Pel, do you have a minute?" Mac asked, as the other angel approached.

The angel appeared mildly surprised to see him, but guided Mac away from the crowded street and into a pleasant looking park.

"What brings you here?" Pel asked curiously as they walked.

"I wanted to ask you something."

"What do you want to know?"

Mac didn't know how his question would be received, particularly bearing in mind they had met just once before, but he was here now and needed to at least try.

"Can you tell me who the demons are who are in relationships with angels?" Mac asked.

Pel stumbled as he missed his footing. "What do you want to know for?"

"There's a human trapped in the Underworld, as a pet of the current Demon King. My partners don't have the power to release him, and I wondered if any of the other demons might."

"I doubt it," Pel replied. "In all honesty, I don't know all the demons who are in relationships with angels. I know one or two — and my own partner, of course — but most are understandably secretive about their relationships. The archangels know, but I doubt they would tell you their identities."

"Damn."

"It's unlikely any of them would have the power to take on the Demon King. My partner certainly doesn't, and she's one of the older demons I know of. The others I know to be lovers of angels are much younger, barely a hundred years old."

"Sometimes age doesn't make a demon powerful," Mac pointed out. "A demon may live a thousand years and still be weak. Do none of them have the power to free this human?"

"None that I know of, and if they do, it's unlikely they'll help."

Mac had suspected this might be the case.

"Can you ask your partner whether she might try?" Mac asked. "Or maybe let me talk to her to ask?"

Pel shook his head. "Sorry, I'm not going to do that. We have an agreement. She doesn't meddle in the affairs of angels, and I don't interfere in the world of demons. Since my assignments generally involve guiding souls rather than thwarting demons, we get along just fine. I'm not going to rock the boat."

"There's a human life at stake here," Mac argued. "An innocent."

"I'm sorry. My partner hasn't the power to take on the Demon King. She has lived as long as she has by keeping her head down and avoiding trouble. She won't go hunting for it, not for a stranger. She's a demon."

"And you're an angel."

"I don't have the power to free this human, you know that. I'm fairly certain you're a more powerful angel than I'll ever be."

"You could at least try. What is it they say, evil triumphs when good men do nothing?"

Pel looked at him steadily. "I pick my battles and need to think about my charges first. I'm not going to get caught up in demon dramas if I don't have to."

Mac felt a surge of frustration but Pel made it clear he wasn't going to budge. It was up to Mac and his lovers to rescue Cody from the Underworld, and they would have to do it on their own.

* * * *

Tristan scrunched up his eyes and concentrated as hard as he could. His inability to change into his demon form frustrated him. He gave himself a rueful smile in the bathroom mirror at the thought. He'd done everything he could to avoid facing the demon, and now he finally needed to do so, he couldn't.

He knew, of course, Alastor would be more than capable of altering his appearance for him, by breaking down the barriers in Tristan's mind, but Alastor would also want to know why Tristan wanted to be in his demon form.

Tristan was well aware of the fact Alastor would not want him going down to the Underworld without him, but he was a little tired of being treated like a child. Ever since the transformation, he had been almost constantly watched by his lovers. The only times they left him alone was when they both went out of the flat on one errand or another. He couldn't really blame them for keeping him under close surveillance. He still cringed when he thought of his first exploration out on his own after becoming an incubus. The all-consuming lust had sent him running back home at a sprint.

That particular episode had triggered the almost constant and stifling supervision by his lovers. Tristan had always been independent and he wanted to do something to clear up his own mess, without Alastor and Mac having to set things right.

Cody was a prisoner in the Underworld because of him. Mac and Alastor had assured him there was plenty of blame to go around, but Tristan knew Cody wouldn't have become involved at all if Tristan hadn't picked him up.

He had to make sure Cody was all right. He didn't think Mac or Alastor would really be bothered about the idea of checking on the human, but he knew they would insist on Alastor accompanying him.

Tristan didn't know whether he wanted to prove himself or was simply rebelling against the constraints of his lovers, but whatever the reason, he'd made the decision to go to the Underworld and visit Cody alone. The problem was his uncooperative demon form didn't want to show itself.

He poured himself a glass of water and took a long swallow. "Okay, Tristan, let's try this again."

Calmer and more relaxed, Tristan leaned on the edge of the counter and tried to imagine his demon form appearing in the mirror before him. "Horns, teeth, hooves," he muttered. "Come on!"

When he opened his eyes, he saw he had failed once again. He glanced down at his bare feet and saw the usual ten toes. The nails on his hands had not extended into claws, his incisors were the same length as always, and there was not so much as a bump on his head where the horns should be.

"Damn it!" he swore as he banged his fist down on the counter.

For a moment he didn't register the pain. Then he realized his anger had triggered something within him and his nails had extended into claws, cutting into the palm of his clenched hand.

"Oh shit." He turned on the tap and shoved his right hand under the cold water, which ran pink with the small stream of blood.

The cuts weren't too bad and the bleeding soon stopped. Tristan dried off his hand and studied his claws with clinical appraisal, trying not to think about the fact they were a part of him.

A knock on the door drew him away from his contemplation.

"Tristan, are you in there?" Mac sounded concerned.

"Yeah," Tristan called back. "I thought you'd gone for a job interview?"

"I did," Mac answered. "That was a couple of hours ago. Are you okay in there?"

Tristan looked at the clock on the bathroom wall. *Where has the morning gone?* "I'm fine."

"Are you sure?"

"Yes. I'll be out in a minute."

Tristan willed his finger nails to return to normal, but just as he had struggled to get his demon side to show itself, now he couldn't make it disappear. "For fuck's sake."

"Tristan?" Mac tried the door handle. "What's going on in there?"

"Nothing."

"Why's the door locked?"

"Habit?" Tristan hadn't meant his reply to sound like a question.

Mac materialized in front of him. "A rather pointless one, all things considered, wouldn't you say?"

Tristan sighed and leaned back against the counter. "There's no privacy in this place."

Mac raised an eyebrow. "And why would you want privacy?"

"Everyone needs some time on their own now and again."

Mac folded his arms across his chest and waited. Tristan knew it would be pointless to continue to try to hide what had happened. He raised his hand to show Mac his clawed fingers.

"Oh, Tristan." Mac pulled him into his arms and wrapped him in a hug. "I know you think your demon side is something to be ashamed of, but you never need to hide it from me."

Mac clearly had the wrong end of the stick and Tristan didn't bother to correct him. He felt a twinge of guilt when Mac stepped back and raised Tristan's clawed hand to his lips, kissing each finger in turn.

Tristan let Mac guide him from the bathroom and into the bedroom.

"Did I ever tell you about when I was alive?" Mac asked, as he made himself comfortable on the bed.

"Bits and pieces." Tristan snuggled up against Mac's side.

"I was something of a freak back then," Mac explained. "People back in those days were much shorter than they are in modern times, but in appearance I was much as I am now. I stood taller by a head than anyone I knew and when people looked up to me, it was because of that. I used to bang my head on the doorjambs when I entered rooms and constantly brushed cobwebs from my hair from being so close to the ceiling."

Tristan couldn't keep back his chuckles, earning him a soft smack on his arse.

"It might be funny now, but back then I felt self-conscious and a freak."

"I can't imagine you being bothered by what people think."

"Not now, but I was then. I would have given anything to be shorter. Now I realize it was meant to be that way. The human race has grown taller and taller over the centuries. As an angel, I never change and now I'm just about average."

"Not quite," Tristan teased. "You're still taller than me and Alastor."

Mac poked him in the ribs. "Thanks for the reminder, shrimp. Anyway, the point I'm making is, even though I felt out of place during my human life, it was because this was my destiny. And even though you don't like your demon side and reject it as much as you can, it's still a part of you and it's there for a reason. You might not know why until many years have passed, but one day it'll all make sense."

Tristan nodded against Mac's chest. As much as he hated what he had become, he had to stop rejecting his demon side.

He closed his eyes and tried to force himself to accept the truth of his destiny. He didn't even need to open his eyes again to know the change had taken place.

"My beautiful, golden demon," Mac whispered.

For the first time, Tristan believed his words and didn't try to argue. If Mac thought him beautiful then it must be true, because his angel wouldn't lie to him about something like that.

Now all Tristan had to do was wait until the opportunity arose for him to slip down into the Underworld and find Cody.

* * * *

Tristan had no idea which way to go when he arrived in the Underworld. He didn't know where the Demon King would keep his so-called pet. Tristan had vague visions of Cody sitting at the steps of the dais while the Demon King held court. Not that it would help if he knew for sure Cody was there. He didn't have a clue which way to go. He wished something in the cavern he had arrived in looked familiar. Even though he had been there before, he already felt lost. All the tunnels seemed the same—dark and forbidding.

There were many demons arriving in the cavern and all of them seemed comfortable in their surroundings. Tristan wished even one of them appeared approachable, but none of them would meet his eye. He would have thought perhaps they had a problem with him, his strange coloring making him self-conscious, but they seemed to be aloof with each other too. There didn't seem to be any trust amongst the demons. They all moved about with their heads down, unwilling to engage with anyone else. Tristan tried to catch the eye of one of the smaller demons and was rewarded with a sharp-toothed snarl for his efforts. Eventually he gave up trying to find someone to help him. He picked one of the tunnels at random and started walking down it. Several demons headed down that particular tunnel, and he followed after them.

The twisting tunnel was lit at intervals by flames that didn't so much chase away the shadows as highlight the sort of horrors to be found in them. Tristan poked his head into one tunnel heading off the main branch and recoiled in horror when he saw a lizard the size of a horse snapping its jaws at a demon who had ventured too far into the lizard's domain.

After that, Tristan decided to stick to the main route and hope for the best.

Eventually, all the demons who had entered the tunnel around the same time as him had drifted off down one route or another, leaving Tristan to continue on his own. He didn't know where he was or whether he was even making any progress. For all he knew, he had spent all this time walking round in circles.

He sat down and leaned against the wall of the tunnel. Perhaps trying to track down Cody had been a bad idea after all. He closed his eyes and tried to concentrate on returning home, but before he knew it he had fallen fast asleep.

The dream that came to him was like nothing he had ever had before. He was walking down these same tunnels, except this time he knew where to go. His feet moved with purpose as they navigated the Underworld with ease. Eventually he arrived at a small cavern and saw Cody curled up in the corner of the sparsely-furnished cave. Cody opened his eyes and stared directly at Tristan. His eyes glowed demon red and Tristan woke with a start.

Tristan scrambled to his feet and set off down the tunnel again, doing his best to recall the direction he had taken in his dream. His progress was fast and sure, and he soon arrived at the entrance to the cave where he'd seen Cody. He hovered at the opening for several moments, wondering whether he should knock on the wall or something. Finally he poked his head into the cave. Cody was there, sitting on a thin mattress, reading a book. He acknowledged Tristan when he walked into the room, and although his eyes were not those of a demon, they flashed with anger.

"Fuck off," he snapped at Tristan before turning back to his book.

"No," Tristan said. "I'm here to check you're doing okay and I'm not leaving until we've talked."

"I'm a prisoner in Hell, thanks to you," Cody answered with venom. "How do you think I'm doing?"

Tristan winced. "I'd give anything to be able to get you out of here. I'm working on a rescue plan."

Cody expression was one of disbelief. "I've been down here for years, how about you try a little harder? I can't even hope to die of old age because I'm not aging."

Tristan wasn't sure whether it would be worth trying to explain how time worked in the Underworld, but he decided to give it a shot. "It's not been so long in the real world."

"This world seems pretty real to me," Cody interrupted.

"You know what I mean—on Earth. It's not been years there, not even months."

Cody tossed his book aside. "I don't give a fuck. You left me here to save your own skin."

"It wasn't like that."

"Then how was it?"

"I didn't have a choice. The Demon King is the most powerful demon of them all. You were the price he demanded for his help."

"I'm not a bargaining chip," Cody yelled. "I'm a human being. I had a life and you stole it from me."

"I'm sorry."

"Sorry doesn't cut it."

Tristan felt his temper begin to rise. Cody didn't understand how difficult it was for him. Unfortunately while he was as angry as this Tristan had virtually no chance of having a reasonable discussion about the best course of action. "I'm doing my best here. I'm trying to find a way to get you home."

Cody glared at him. "Try harder."

Tristan stepped toward the exit and cast a quick glance over his shoulder. "I *will* get you out of here."

Cody picked up his book again and flipped over the page. "Sure you will," he muttered with obvious sarcasm. "Tell me Tristan, how do you sleep at night, knowing what you've done?"

Tristan frowned, not so much at the question itself, but at Cody's tone. Something in his voice told Tristan he knew the answer to the question already.

"What do you mean by that?" Tristan asked.

Cody shrugged. "Just a simple question."

"Was it?"

Cody gave him a not entirely pleasant smile. "Pleasant dreams, Tristan." Then he turned back to his book once more.

Tristan left with the uneasy feeling Cody might be behind his recent nightmare. The question was how a human, a prisoner of the Demon King, had managed to obtain the power to invade his dreams.

Chapter Ten

Tristan hid in the woods, shielded by a large boulder and some extremely prickly bushes. Someone chased after him and he knew it would be bad if they found him.

The rain poured down and even though the trees sheltered him a little, they couldn't do much to keep him dry after so many hours of running.

"Be still my love," a familiar voice murmured into his ear. Again the language in his dream was strange, yet at the same time, perfectly comprehensible.

Tristan watched Mac as he peered over the boulder.

"We should have been more careful." Mac sat back down.

Tristan had no idea what he was talking about. "Where are we?" he asked.

"Too close to the settlement," Mac muttered. "We'll try to put some distance between us and them once night has fallen."

"Settlement?"

Mac looked at him askance. "Duach, are you well?"

Suddenly the memory of what had happened crashed over Tristan like a wave. Their encounter in the trees, the woman who was apparently his wife, and their brutal and public punishment.

"Duach?" Mac shifted round to sit behind him. "You're bleeding again."

Tristan had wondered what the dampness running down his spine was. He had thought it was water from the heavy rain.

Mac carefully eased Tristan's tunic away from his back. "Let me see."

Tristan could tell from the sharp intake of breath it wasn't a pretty sight. "How bad is it?"

"You'll live," Mac teased. "I'll accept no other alternative."

"You might not have a say in it," Tristan reminded him, hissing as the falling rain hit his bare back. "They want us dead."

"It matters not. I want you alive."

Tristan wrapped his arms around his knees and let Mac tend to his wounds. He tried not to flinch at Mac's ministrations, but the pain made him sick to his stomach and what little food they had managed to scavenge during their flight from the village felt like a rock in his gut.

"Why are they so angry with us?" Tristan asked. "Is it just because I betrayed my wife? Or was it because I enjoy what you do to me?"

"I don't know," Mac admitted. "I've never known anything other than life in the village. No other men there seek pleasure with their own kind."

"Why are we different?"

"I don't know. Did you enjoy bedding your wife?"

Tristan didn't have any recollection of taking his wife, or any woman for that matter, to his bed.

"You can tell me the truth, Duach," Mac said. "I know what we have together is stronger than anything I've ever known before. Is it the same for you?"

"Yes. Never doubt my feelings for you."

"I never do. Not since the first time we touched. Do you remember that day?"

"*Remind me,*" Tristan replied. "*Talk to me while you're tending my back and it'll take my mind off things.*"

"*It was last summer. You'd gone to collect firewood and I followed you out to the trees. You strayed far into the woods, as far as the stream. You decided to bathe in the waters.*"

"*That sounds nice.*"

"*You took off your garments and stepped into the water.*"

"*What were you doing while I bathed?*"

"*Watching you.*"

"*Was that all?*"

"*No.*"

Tristan smiled to himself. "*What else?*"

"*I touched myself.*"

"*Had you done that before?*"

"*Yes, of course.*"

"*While you thought of me?*"

"*Not really. I thought of faceless, nameless people at such times.*"

"*Men?*"

Mac was quiet for a moment. "*Yes.*"

"*Did you never think of women?*"

"*Thinking of women never produced the same effect as thinking of men. And after seeing you, thinking of any other man was equally pointless.*"

"*You've never bedded a woman?*"

"*No. That's why I wonder whether what you shared with your wife made you happy. Would you have been better off staying with her?*"

"*No.*"

"*You'd have a home and a family, a roof over your head, food in your belly, and no open wounds on your back and thighs.*"

"*I can live without those things, and I can put up with the pain,*" Tristan whispered. "*I can't live without you.*"

Mac's hand stilled on his back.

A small sound drew Tristan's attention away from Mac. A figure stood directly in front of them, just a few feet away. For a moment he thought it was one of their pursuers, then he realized his mistake.

"Pleasant dreams?" Cody asked, before turning and walking away.

Tristan shivered and leaned into Mac. He wanted to wake up and he wanted to wake now.

* * * *

Tristan didn't know whether to feel disappointed or relieved his suspicion about Cody had been proved to be correct. Seeing him in his dream made it clear Cody was definitely involved. He tried to feel anger toward the human, but all he felt was guilt at driving him to do this. He just wished he knew how Cody had gained such powers.

Mac and Alastor still slept and Tristan eased his way out from between them, needing a little time on his own to gather his thoughts.

"Where are you going?" Mac asked, as Tristan reached the door. "Are you okay?"

Tristan gestured for Mac to be quiet, lest he wake Alastor too. He hoped Mac would go back to sleep, but his angel could clearly tell something was wrong and he followed Tristan into the living room.

Mac sat Tristan down on the sofa and went to make them each a coffee. "What is it?" he asked as he passed Tristan a steaming mug. "And don't try fobbing me off."

Tristan gave a small smile. Mac knew him so well. "It's Cody."

Mac sipped on his coffee and waited for Tristan to continue.

"He's the one behind my dreams," Tristan explained.

"Dreams? I thought it was just the one."

Tristan couldn't meet Mac's eye. "No, I just had another one. It wasn't quite as bad as the first, but neither were particularly pleasant."

"And you think Cody might be behind them?"

"He is."

"Cody's a human," Mac pointed out. "He doesn't have that sort of power."

"He must have some sort of help."

"What makes you so sure he's behind them?"

"I just saw him in my dream," Tristan explained. "And I..."

"What?" Mac prompted as Tristan's voice trailed off.

"I visited him in the Underworld."

Mac put his coffee aside and folded his arms across his chest. "When was this?"

"Yesterday."

"And you kept this from me?"

Tristan took a drink of his coffee to avoid looking Mac in the eye. "I knew you wouldn't approve."

"Damn right. I can't believe you and Alastor didn't tell me."

"Alastor doesn't know I went down there," Tristan clarified. "I knew he'd be as pissed off as you."

Tristan could tell Mac was annoyed with him. His wings, mostly invisible when he was on Earth, had appeared with his loss of control and they were a dark gray, a sure sign of his anger.

"Why did you do something so stupid as to go down there without Alastor to protect you?"

Tristan's own temper flared at the reprimand. "I'm not a child. I'm perfectly capable of taking care of myself. I wanted to check on Cody, and I did. I don't have to report my every move to the two of you."

"You could have been trapped down there, taken prisoner or tortured."

"But I wasn't."

"That's not the point. And Alastor would agree with me."

Tristan sprang from his seat and stalked across the room. "Of course he would. You both take sides against me when it comes to letting me make my own decisions. The two of you treat me like a child and it's starting to piss me off. I'm not your pet."

Mac reeled back. "We don't think of you like that."

"Don't you? You and Alastor have been around for centuries and I'm the *baby*. Well, I'm sick of being treated like one."

Tristan's voice had risen during their argument and had apparently been loud enough to wake Alastor, who stood in the doorway of the bedroom, an expression of hurt on his face.

"I won't call you baby if you really don't like it," Alastor said. "I never meant to make you feel like you weren't equal to the two of us."

Tristan regretted his words. "You can call me whatever you like." He wrapped his arms around Alastor's neck. "Insensitive idiot would probably be ideal right now."

Alastor didn't hug him back and when Tristan stepped back he could tell from the expressions flying across Alastor's face that Mac was filling him in telepathically on the parts of the conversation he had missed.

"Idiot is right," Alastor finally replied. "You went to the Underworld without me? What the fuck were you thinking?"

Tristan stamped his way back to the sofa and threw himself onto the leather. "I thought I'd make sure Cody was okay. Sorry if my showing a bit of initiative hurts your ego."

Alastor and Mac continued to talk privately, while Tristan became more and more irate at their excluding him from the discussion.

"I *am* right here, you know," he snapped. "Would you stop talking about me like I'm not in the room?"

Mac sighed and Alastor took a seat in the armchair.

"Okay, let's see what we can sort out," Mac said. "Tristan, neither of us thinks of you as a child."

Tristan opened his mouth to argue, but Mac raised his hand to stall his protest. "We don't. But we do have a number of centuries experience in dealing with demons and we've got a lot more knowledge of the Underworld. You have no idea of the danger you placed yourself in by going down there.

"We love you, and the thought of you putting yourself in danger like this worries us. What if you were taken prisoner down there? What if you got lost and couldn't get back home?"

"But I didn't."

"But what if you had?" Mac pressed.

"Alastor would have known how to find me," Tristan pointed out. "Him being an expert on the Underworld."

Alastor snorted from across the room. "Is that what you think?"

"Well, aren't you?"

"Not even close." Tristan could detect a slight hint of amusement in Alastor's eyes. "I venture as far as I must and get out of there as quick as I can. The Underworld is as vast as the Earth itself, and there are many levels I have never sought to travel to. Nor would I want to. You could have been lost to us forever."

"I could teleport back here any time I wanted."

"Not from all of the Underworld," Alastor stated. "The deeper you go, the more dangerous it is. There are places where our powers are weakened as well as demons who can steal your powers from you, leaving you stuck there. You could also have angered the Demon King if you'd run afoul of him and then you'd end up suffering a similar fate to that of Lawrence. There are plenty of ways you could have been trapped there without our knowing."

"But I'm fine," Tristan interrupted. "I didn't come to any harm and I'm home now."

"Yes, you are," Mac agreed. "But next time, you might not be so lucky."

Tristan huffed. "What do you want from me? A promise I'll never go back to the Underworld without Alastor babysitting me?"

"I wouldn't phrase it quite like that, but yes," Mac said.

Tristan turned away from Mac and faced Alastor, who appeared less annoyed and more amused.

"Yes?" Tristan asked. "I can tell you want to say something, so how about you get it over with now?"

Alastor grinned at him. "Just wondering what payment I can expect from Mac for my babysitting duties."

Tristan picked up the nearest thing to hand—the remote for the television—and threw it at Alastor. "I'm glad you find everything so amusing." Still, Tristan couldn't help the small smile forming on his own lips. "Fine, I won't go down to the Underworld without permission from one of you."

"You won't go down without Alastor," Mac amended. "I won't allow you to take chances with your safety."

Tristan agreed reluctantly. "Okay."

Alastor gave them a grim smile. "Now, what's this Mac says about Cody being the one behind your recent dreams?"

Tristan filled Alastor in on his discussions with Cody, the human's parting comment to him, and seeing him in his dream on his return.

"Are you sure he wasn't in your dream just because he's on your mind?" Mac asked.

"Maybe," Tristan admitted. "But I don't think so. I think he was there because he's somehow controlling what I dream about."

"Was Cody still human when you saw him down in the Underworld?" Alastor asked.

"Yes, he appeared to be."

"Are you sure?"

"I think so. His eyes were still normal."

Alastor nodded. "Had he been turned, his eyes would be those of a demon, even if the Demon King let him retain his human body in the Underworld."

"If he's still human, how can he control Tristan's dreams?" Mac asked. "Could the Demon King be helping him?"

Alastor considered Mac's question for several minutes. "I don't know. I can't see why he would consider it worthwhile tormenting Tristan, but then again, I can't see why he would want to bother keeping Cody prisoner either."

"Great, so the Demon King has decided to relieve his boredom by fucking with my head." Tristan rubbed his eyes. "I just want a decent night's sleep. Is that too much to ask for?"

"If it *is* the Demon King targeting you," Alastor reminded him. "It could be another demon entirely."

"But who? And why?"

"A friend of Lawrence's, perhaps?" Mac suggested. "There must be a few demons out there who aren't happy about his imprisonment in the Underworld."

"I can't imagine who," Alastor muttered. "Besides, he'll be freed before too long. It's not as though he's a permanent prisoner down there."

"What do you mean?" Tristan asked.

"Lawrence has just been sent down to the pit to learn his lesson. It's not like he's a danger to the Demon King and he's not been killed."

"Isn't he dead already?"

Alastor shook his head. "The human he once was is dead. The demon lives in his body, the same as it does in mine and yours. Killing the demon would trap him in the Underworld permanently. There's no bargaining their way out for demons who have been killed. Cody's circumstances notwithstanding, since he's very much alive, deceased humans who are sent to Hell have one chance of escaping the Underworld, by turning demon."

"Then demons who are killed just hang around in the Underworld?" Tristan asked. "Sounds like a recipe for trouble, if you ask me. What's to stop them combining forces and taking on the Demon King or something?"

"They have no powers. Even if they managed to defeat him simply by their vast numbers, it would not restore their powers and they would still remain trapped down there."

"Don't they obtain his powers if they kill him?" Mac asked. "I thought that was how it worked with demons?"

"It is, but not for demons who have died. The ability to gain powers in such a way is lost along with the rest of their supernatural skills when a demon dies. There are no second chances to escape the Underworld."

"You mean they don't get another chance at life?" Mac asked. "No rebirth as a mortal?"

"Not that I've ever heard of. Even Lucifer himself didn't get another shot, and if a fallen angel doesn't, then what hope is there for the rest of us? The rules apply to him as much as the rest of us. He'll be down there in the pit somewhere, trapped in the Underworld with the rest of the dead demons."

"Someone actually killed Lucifer?" Tristan asked.

"Yes. It was a long time ago, during the last great war between demons and angels. He fell near the end of the battle. He was defeated by Michael himself."

"The archangel?"

Mac picked up Alastor's tale. "They battled for days, never stopping, even when the rest of the armies had retired for the night. Then in the early hours of what turned out to be the last morning of fighting, Michael returned to our camp to confirm Lucifer had finally been defeated. His words spurred the remaining angels out onto the field one final time to end the war once and for all."

Tristan took a few minutes to process this new information.

"We seem to have strayed from the problem at hand, though," Mac commented. "That being Cody and Tristan's dreams. I think we're all agreed that Cody doesn't have the power to control Tristan's dreams, so he must have help from a demon, either the Demon King or someone else."

"I'm thinking someone else," Alastor said. "I just can't see the Demon King messing with Tristan's mind like this."

From what he had seen of the leader of the Underworld, Tristan was inclined to agree with his assessment.

* * * *

Mac waited for Raphael to answer his call. It would be quicker to go up to the Realm of Angels to speak to him, but he wanted Alastor and Tristan to be present. Finally, some half an hour after Mac had first called for his superior, Raphael appeared in the living room. Mac couldn't recollect a time when he had been forced to seek the counsel of the archangel as frequently as now. He suspected Raphael might be irritated with his constant questions as well, at least if his expression right now was anything to go by.

"You requested my presence?" Raphael asked.

Mac gave a deep and respectful bow. "Thank you for coming. I need your advice once again, please."

Raphael's eyes widened. "It's not as though you've taken my advice in the past." He shot a pointed glance at Alastor.

"Please," Mac begged. "We're worried about Tristan's dreams."

"As you should be," Raphael agreed.

Mac could tell the conversation would be difficult. "Can you tell us, is it the Demon King who's messing with Tristan?"

"You already know from Tristan's enquiries that Cody is the one behind the dreams."

"Cody's human. He doesn't have the power to do this."

"Not alone."

"Then who's helping him, if not the Demon King himself?"

"The Demon King is already bored of his pet. Cody's leash is a long one and he is an attractive human."

"What are you saying?"

Raphael looked at him steadily. "Cody is not alone in the Underworld. He has help in executing his revenge."

"Revenge?" Raphael waited until Mac realized what he meant. "He blames Tristan for leaving him there."

"And Alastor," Raphael confirmed. "He is also angry with you and myself for not saving him."

"Aren't you concerned?" Mac asked. Raphael didn't seem particularly bothered that a human had formed an alliance with a demon to take revenge on them.

"He cannot touch me," Raphael stated. "He hasn't that sort of power, even with the help he has right now."

"But he can hurt the rest of us," Mac pointed out. "Is that what you want?"

"I want nothing of the sort. I have no wish to see one of my most compassionate angels hurt."

"But you don't mind seeing Tristan suffer," Alastor interrupted.

Raphael looked down his nose at him with a stern frown. "I cannot interfere directly with what is meant to be."

"Can you at least tell us who's helping Cody torture Tristan—or better yet, tell us how we can block whoever it is from Tristan's dreams."

"There's no way to block a dream demon from entering the mind of anyone who sleeps."

Mac had heard of dream demons and mentally chided himself for not having considered the possibility before now. "Who has that sort of power?"

"There are many demons with such power as well as a few angels."

"Angels have the power to control dreams?" Tristan asked.

Raphael turned to Alastor and Tristan sitting beside each other on the sofa. "Very few of them, but there are angels who help those whose sleep is troubled, soothing them and ensuring pleasant dreams. Others inspire the gifted through dreams and visions. Of course, your question is not about the angels with this power, is it?"

"No," Mac agreed. "What demons do you know of?"

"There are many dream demons. Some bring nightmares to sleepers. Others whisper of temptation and seek to corrupt." Raphael shot a glare at Alastor, making it plain to everyone what he thought of the latter.

"Is there a possibility these aren't just regular dreams?" Mac asked quietly, earning twin glances of surprise from Alastor and Tristan.

"What do you mean?" Raphael queried.

"Could they be Tristan's past life memories?"

Raphael appeared to give the matter some thought and he paced the room for several minutes. "It's possible, I suppose. But how do you know they aren't just exceptionally vivid dreams inspired by a book, a painting, or even a modern television program? Past life memories, when accessed, are far more real to a person than mere dreams."

"These *do* seem more vivid than anything I've dreamt before," Tristan commented. "I could still feel the pain of what happened in the dreams when I woke up."

"That doesn't mean they're memories."

"But it could?"

"Yes, it could, but I think it unlikely."

"I'm in his dreams," Mac said. "You told me we've known each other before. That's why I wonder if his dreams are something more."

"Just because you're in his dreams, it doesn't mean Tristan is starting to remember a past life."

Mac pressed on, "Hypothetically, if Tristan is remembering a past life, and if they aren't just dreams, who would have that sort of power?"

Raphael sat in one of the leather chairs and rested his chin on the tips of his index fingers. "Not a lesser dream demon, that's certain. The least powerful of their kind seek out a person's fear and turn their dreams to nightmares."

"My dreams are nightmares," Tristan muttered.

Raphael acknowledged he had heard him. "The more powerful of the dream demons would have the power to do what you suggest, as well as any individual demon with direct access to Tristan's memories."

"What do you mean by direct access?" Tristan asked.

"To access the memories in your mind takes a great deal of power. If a demon had your memories in their possession it would not require as much skill to return them to you as you sleep."

"How can we find out for sure what's happening?" Tristan asked.

Raphael closed his eyes and Tristan gave a small yelp.

"What is it?" Alastor asked as Tristan jumped and glared at the archangel.

"I was checking your mind," Raphael replied.

"And?"

"Your guess is correct, Machidiel. Some of Tristan's past life memories are not in his head. There are gaps there."

"How is that possible?" Tristan asked.

"When you became a demon, your memories were taken by the one who made you," Raphael reminded him.

"And I bargained for them to be returned," Tristan replied.

"Could Lawrence have kept some, or all, of Tristan's past life memories for himself?" Mac asked.

"Lawrence does not have the power to meddle with Tristan's mind in this manner," Raphael told them. "But he might be a place to start your enquiries. I would suggest acting quickly."

"If we can't stop the demon, when will it end?" Mac wasn't sure he wanted to know the answer to the question, yet he had to ask.

Raphael shrugged. "It'll end when Tristan has been shown everything there is to see."

"Like we couldn't have figured that out for ourselves," Alastor snapped.

"Then you should have no trouble in figuring out everything else you need to know, too," Raphael snarled back. "Instead of tearing me away from my duties to sort out your mess."

"I'm sorry," Mac hurried to reassure Raphael. "Alastor's just worried about Tristan, as am I."

Raphael rose to leave. "Any demon in possession of Tristan's memories could be the one you are searching for. But you might narrow your search by making enquiries of one of the more powerful dream demons. They will know if any other demon has been learning their ways and treading their paths in recent weeks. Infiltrating dreams is an easy skill to learn, but learn it, they must. If Lawrence, for example, is the demon you seek, the leaders of the dream demons will know of his recent foray into their world."

"What if the one we seek already has those skills?" Alastor asked. "It could be a dream demon itself."

"Then enquiring of the dream demons would be the first place to start, wouldn't it?" Raphael asked with a fair amount of sarcasm. "Now, if you'll excuse me, I *do* have other angels to supervise. I have already given you far more information than you deserve."

Raphael disappeared from the room without saying goodbye, appearing even more irritated than he had been on his arrival.

"He gets more and more unpleasant every time I see him," Alastor muttered. "What is his problem?"

Before Mac or Tristan could answer him, a second archangel entered the room.

"Michael." Mac greeted him with another bow.

"Machidiel," Michael said. "Alastor, Tristan."

"Were you listening in?" Alastor asked.

"Yes," Michael confirmed without any trace of guilt. "Machidiel, if I could speak with you privately for a moment please?"

Mac gestured for Alastor and Tristan to remain inside while he led the archangel to the rooftop garden.

"Your relationship with Raphael is becoming more strained every time you meet," Michael commented once they were alone.

"I know." Mac sighed and sat down on the metal garden bench.

"Conflicts between the two of you won't help when the time to vote on Raguel's petition arrives."

"I know that, too. What do you suggest I do when I need advice? Raphael is my direct superior. I'm supposed to turn to him for help."

"Perhaps until the voting takes place, you'd consider asking *me* for advice?" Michael suggested.

"You don't think turning to you might anger him just as much?" Mac asked.

Michael sat down beside him and patted his thigh reassuringly. "I suspect whatever we do will make little difference to Raphael's decision."

"Unless what I do is leave Alastor and Tristan and give up on my mission to save them."

"Until you believe you can save them, you never will," Michael commented, before vanishing from the garden, leaving Mac alone with his thoughts.

Chapter Eleven

Tristan stumbled into the kitchen, feeling unrested and irritable. Once again his sleep had been plagued with nightmares of homophobic villagers chasing him and Mac from village to village. As a gay man who had had life relatively easy with nothing more than the occasional sneering jibe from narrow-minded idiots whose opinions he didn't care about, it had been unsettling to dream of being treated as some kind of pariah.

Alastor sat at the table and Tristan grabbed a slice of toast as he joined him.

"Sleep well?" Alastor asked.

"No," Tristan muttered between bites. "These dreams are getting worse every night."

Alastor squeezed his hand and Tristan tried to pluck up the courage to say what he needed to.

"I've decided to go and see Lawrence," he managed to blurt in between gulps of his coffee.

Alastor choked on his own drink and Tristan reached over to bang his back with his fist. "What the fuck for?" Alastor finally gasped.

"I want to know why he kept the memories of my past life from me."

"We don't even know for sure he did. And I really wouldn't recommend going down into the pit. It's one big torture chamber and I don't think you're ready to see that."

"I don't think I'd ever be ready to see something so vile," Tristan said. "But if it's the only way to find out for certain, I'm sure I'll survive."

"You don't have to do this. There's no point in questioning Lawrence. He's a prisoner down there. He wouldn't have the power to infiltrate your dreams, even if he were free. And why would Cody combine forces with him? He saw him with you in LA and must surely blame him as much as he does the rest of us."

"But no one else has ever had my memories in their possession."

"I doubt Lawrence has them now. They're probably long gone."

"But gone where? If Lawrence did keep them from me, this is our one lead as to who might be helping Cody."

"We could question the leader of the dream demons, as Raphael suggested."

"Do you really think he'll help us?" Tristan's tone made it clear he didn't believe it was worth the effort of even asking.

"No, but what else can we do?"

"We can question Lawrence. I have to find out what he knows, and at least we know where he is right now. Seems to me like it's a good time to try and get the truth out of him." He wasn't going to let Alastor talk him out of this.

"Fine," Alastor begrudgingly agreed. "We'll leave as soon as Mac returns."

"No. I'm going alone."

Alastor grabbed hold of his arm. "You promised you wouldn't go down there without me."

"I know, but like *you* said, it's not good to show weakness in front of other demons."

"You're using my own words against me."

Tristan grinned. "You know I have a point. I just need you to tell me which way to go when I arrive."

"And if I don't?"

"Then I'll be wandering around for heaven knows how long and may never find Lawrence or make it back."

Alastor loosened his grip on Tristan's arm. "Promise me you'll come straight home after you find him."

"Of course."

Alastor glared at him. "I mean it, Tristan. I don't know what scares me more, the idea of you alone in the Underworld, or the thought of telling Mac where you are when he returns."

"I'll probably be back before Mac anyway. Now, can you write down the directions to the torture chambers for me?"

Alastor reluctantly agreed and grabbed a pen and paper. "When you arrive in the Underworld, find the tunnel with a carving of a bird above the entrance. Take that route and don't deviate from the main path. Whenever you reach a fork in the tunnel, take the one sloping downward. You'll reach the pit eventually, and believe me, you'll know when you've got there."

"Thank you." Tristan left Alastor with a quick kiss goodbye. When he didn't return immediately Alastor wished he had ever been a patient man.

* * * *

"You let him go where?" Mac couldn't believe his ears.

"I didn't *let* him go anywhere. He's a grown man. He wanted to go and speak with Lawrence."

"Why isn't he back yet? Something must have happened to him. Go and find him."

Alastor didn't move from his place on the sofa. "He'll come back when he's done. I'm not going to chase him round the Underworld like a lost puppy. It would show him as weak to the other demons down there."

"I don't care what the other demons think of him. I want him back here where he's safe."

Alastor disappeared from the room without a word. Mac wasn't sure whether he had gone to find Tristan or not. He realized he could have handled the situation better than he had.

* * * *

Alastor nursed his pint as he considered the clock above the bar. It would be an impossible task to find Tristan in the Underworld. Mac had no idea of the vastness of the torture chambers. Tristan would return when he'd finished his enquiries. He had directions and Alastor trusted him to stick to them.

"Can I join you?"

Alastor looked up and groaned when he saw the archangel Michael hovering over him. "If you like."

Michael sat at the table and gazed at Alastor thoughtfully.

"Did you want something?" Alastor asked.

"Just a little chat."

"You want a *chat* with *me*?"

"Is that so difficult to believe?"

"Don't you have something more important to be doing?"

"What makes you think my talking to you *isn't* important?"

The first thing to pop into Alastor's mind was perhaps this was some sort of trap. Archangels didn't just pop down the pub for a beer and a chat with demons. He scanned the pub for other angels, finding just one other present, a young woman near the bar. Alastor breathed a sigh of relief that hers was the single angelic aura in the place, before he realized he couldn't see Michael's aura. Had the archangel given up his wings? Surely he wouldn't have done such a thing? Still, try as he might, Alastor could not see the heavenly aura that normally surrounded an angel. It wasn't there. No glow, not even so much as a spark to reveal him as an angel.

"Have you finished?" Michael asked with amusement.

"Why don't you have an aura?" Alastor blurted.

"I do, but I usually choose to keep it hidden when I'm on Earth."

"You can do that?"

"Of course, all angels can."

Alastor felt a little dense at Michael's revelation.

"You shouldn't continue to blame yourself for Machidiel's decision to sacrifice his life when Tristan turned. You couldn't have known he'd given up his wings."

"I don't blame myself."

"Lie to me if you wish, but don't lie to yourself."

Alastor took another drink of his beer and turned away.

"Don't you want to know why I'm here?" Michael asked.

"Not really."

"You're not even a tiny bit curious?"

Alastor slammed his glass onto the table. "Fine, why are you here?"

His flash of temper didn't seem to faze Michael at all. "I wanted to talk to you about Tristan."

"What about him?"

"You have noticed he is unexpectedly powerful."

"Do you lot have nothing better to do with eternity than spy on us?"

Michael ignored his question. "I'm not your enemy."

"You're an archangel."

"I'm not Raphael. I hold no personal grudge against you."

"So he *does* hate me in particular."

Michael took a drink before he answered. "Raphael recruited Machidiel. He sees his relationship with you as a personal insult."

"Our relationship has nothing to do with him."

"No, but he doesn't see things the same way. Machidiel has always followed Raphael's orders and advice, except when it comes to you. From the moment he met you, Machidiel has been at odds with Raphael."

"And Raphael blames me for it."

"Yes."

Alastor snorted. At least Michael didn't sugar-coat the truth. "Do *you* blame me?"

"I'm not so close to the situation. I can see things more clearly than Raphael."

"So you *do* blame me." Alastor took a long drink of his beer. Most demons managed to saunter through their lives without drawing the attention of a single angel. Trust him to have not one, but two archangels gunning for him.

"No, actually, I don't. Your relationship with Machidiel and Tristan was always going to happen. Nothing could have prevented the three of you coming together."

Alastor frowned at Michael. "What makes you so sure?"

"Because some things are meant to be. Tristan has not remembered you yet, but he will soon dream of the time he once knew you."

"Tristan knew me in the life he's remembering?"

"Yes."

"What happened to us?"

"If you don't stop the dream demon, you'll no doubt find out. I would suggest you make every effort to end Tristan's nightmares before that happens."

Alastor supposed he shouldn't have expected anything useful from an archangel. "Is that all you wanted to say?"

"No. Like I said, I wanted to talk to you about Tristan."

"What about him?"

"You have already discovered he's immune to your powers of persuasion."

"Yes. What of it?"

"He also has unusual coloring in his demon form."

"Do you want to get to the fucking point?"

Michael went quiet and Alastor wondered if he had pissed him off a little too much. "Sorry, go on."

Michael smiled. "Look around you and tell me what you see."

"What?"

"Look around the pub and tell me what you see."

Alastor was losing patience but did as Michael said. He didn't know what he should be searching for. He could see nothing except the female angel at the bar. "I see the other angel sitting at the end of the bar."

"Very good, but I'm the only angel here."

Alastor turned to Michael. "What?"

"Marissa is not an angel, at least not any more. She gave up her wings to live a mortal life a little over three years ago."

"Why would she do that?"

"For love."

"Why does she still have an angelic aura if she's human?"

"As an angel, she could hide it, as any of us can. As a human, she no longer has the ability to do so. What you see is not merely an aura, it's the source of our powers. As a human, she cannot tap into that power, but it's still there. The aura is a sign of those who are, or have once been angels."

"Why are you telling me this?"

"When Tristan fed from Machidiel that first time, Machidiel was human, but his aura remained. Had you thought to scan him for it, you would have seen it as surely as you see hers now. Machidiel could not have hidden it from you. Tristan fed from an angel's power as he completed his transformation."

Alastor tried to piece together what Michael was telling him. "I don't understand."

"Even though Machidiel was human, he retained the powers he had as an angel when Tristan fed from him. The reason Tristan is able to block your powers is because he drained a former angel that night."

"Then he doesn't have some natural resistance to my powers?"

"No, he is far more powerful than both you and Machidiel, because of who he feeds from."

"Is that why he couldn't feed from Cody? His body craves more powerful sustenance."

"No. He can feed from anyone he wishes, though he would find it difficult to sustain himself on humans alone. His own morals and sense of right and wrong prevented him from feeding on Cody. Feeding from Machidiel at the point of his transformation is also the reason for his unusual coloring."

"Does anyone else know about this?"

"The other archangels are aware."

"Why are you telling me this?"

"Because you need to know Tristan can take care of himself."

"I already know that. If I didn't, I'd be chasing him round the Underworld now, just like Mac wanted me to."

"Just make sure you remember."

Alastor nodded, but Michael had already vanished. Alastor supposed as archangels went, Michael wasn't as bad as some of the others.

* * * *

Tristan wandered the Underworld searching for Lawrence. Alastor's instructions had led him as far as the main torture chamber, but now Tristan was on his own. Every now and then he was forced to ask for directions, and was pointed toward yet another winding tunnel, each as bleak and foreboding as the one before.

The path he followed seemed to be on a steady downward incline and the farther he went, the louder the screams seemed to become.

The initial chilliness of the caverns became warmer as his journey progressed. The dampness turned muggy and when he peered into some of the tunnels off the path he walked, he could just make out flames flickering in the distance. More than anything he wanted to go home and forget all about seeing Lawrence. The slim hope his memories might be the key to releasing Cody from his imprisonment kept him going.

Tristan cringed as he slowly picked his way through the demons and the human souls they tormented. He knew Alastor had spent time down here, both as the torturer and the tortured. Tristan hoped he was never called on to be the former because he didn't think his stomach could take it.

Everywhere around him, humans cried out for mercy. Nowhere could Tristan see a demon being tortured.

"Lost?" a large demon with an unpleasant grin asked him as he wielded a whip with ease and efficiency.

Tristan jumped back as the whip cracked again. It came a little too close for comfort. "I'm trying to find Lawrence, an incubus who's down here."

"Incubus, huh?" The demon stepped back and scratched his chest thoughtfully. "Don't get many of them down here. This here's the torture chamber and an incubus isn't much good at that kind of thing."

"He's not a torturer," Tristan clarified. "The king sent him down here for punishment."

"You need the next level, down there." The demon pointed to the center of the chamber where the top of a ladder was just visible at the edge of the hole in the floor.

Tristan thanked him and hurried on his way.

The ladder was long and he could barely see the bottom as he stepped onto the first rung. He climbed down, struggling to maintain a grip on the rungs with his hooves. He soon found himself in another chamber, this one smaller than the previous one, yet equally packed with demons.

A quick inquiry with the nearest demon saw him pointed in the direction of one of the many antechambers and it was there where he finally found Lawrence.

When he first saw the dazed expression on Lawrence's face, he thought perhaps he might be too far gone in pain to answer his questions. Luckily for Tristan, the demon's fast recovery was soon apparent.

"Come to gloat?" Lawrence asked. He sat up from the stone bench he had been chained to and grasped for the nearby water, but found it was just out of his reach. The demon who had been torturing him chuckled as he stood back against the wall.

Tristan wondered whether to pass Lawrence the water or whether doing such a thing would result in him joining him down there for punishment of his own. He decided not to risk it.

"I wanted to ask you about the memories you took from me," Tristan began.

"I gave you your bloody memories back," Lawrence snapped. "Is life with your fuck buddies not living up to your recollections?"

Tristan folded his arms across his chest. "I'm not talking about the memories of my current life. I want to know about the memories of my past life, the ones you kept back."

For a moment Tristan had the pleasure of seeing Lawrence appear as stunned as he had ever seen him. His guess had been accurate. He was sure now he had deliberately kept the memories and had never believed Tristan would notice. He recovered quickly and shrugged in an offhand manner.

"What use were they to you? It's not like you could remember them."

"You had no right to keep them. Our bargain was for the return of my memories, remember?"

"I remember. Perhaps you should have been more specific."

"Why didn't you give them back to me with the rest?" Tristan asked.

"I gave you most of your past life memories back. I just kept the ones from the life where you knew *them*."

Tristan didn't need to ask who they were, Lawrence meant Alastor and Mac. "But what good are those memories to you?"

Lawrence waved a hand airily. "Bargaining chips amongst demons. You and your lovers were rather active and X-rated memories are highly valuable down here. This break in my torture, which I'm wasting answering your pointless questions, was paid for with the memory of a night I spent with a rather attractive set of twins in Venice at the turn of the eighteenth century."

Tristan didn't want to hear about Lawrence's past conquests. "Who has my memories now?"

"No idea," Lawrence answered cheerily. "I used them to pay for this lovely private chamber you see before you. The antechambers are a little cooler than the main room and the torturers in them are far more open to bribes."

Tristan shoved Lawrence as hard as he could. "You're telling me you kept my memories just to get yourself a better deal down here?"

Lawrence laughed. "No. I didn't plan on being sent down here. I kept them because I could."

"Who did you trade them to? Was it a dream demon?"

"No, just a regular demon who has probably traded them on again already. Your memories are long gone, so you might as well forget about getting them back. Now, why don't you run along and let the good demon over there get back to work?"

"Not yet." Tristan raised his hand to halt the demon who had taken a step forward, eager to resume his torture. "One more question."

The torturer stood still. "Make it quick."

Tristan turned back to Lawrence. "Is there anything in my past life memories that can be used to hurt us?"

"You and me?" Lawrence asked with mock innocence.

"Me and my lovers," Tristan clarified stonily. "I need to know what happened to us."

Lawrence howled with laughter. "You died, of course. You all died and moved on. Who fucking cares what happened to you thousands of years ago? Don't you think you have enough problems in this life?"

"Tell me," Tristan demanded.

Lawrence finally stopped laughing and wiped the tears of mirth from his eyes. "I don't know. I *really* don't know. I didn't go through all your memories, just enough of them to judge their value down here. Only the demon who has them now can answer your questions."

The torturer turned to Tristan. "Would you like me to check he's telling the truth?" He pulled a set of spiked chains from the wall and checked them for strength. "If he's lying, I'll soon find out."

Tristan stumbled back toward the entrance, shaking his head. "No. I believe him."

The torturer raised an eyebrow, his expression one of doubt, but he took Tristan at his word. "As you wish." He then turned back to Lawrence, and Tristan closed his eyes so he couldn't see what happened next. Lawrence's scream rang in his ears as he transported himself from the antechamber to the penthouse.

* * * *

Mac rushed to his side the moment Tristan appeared in the living room. "I've been so worried about you. I thought you'd been kept down there." Tristan let himself be pulled into the angel's arms and held tightly.

"I don't understand." Tristan checked the clock and saw it was late evening. "I thought I'd come back to the same time I left."

Mac shook his head. "Providing you control your return, you can come back to any time you wish. If another demon sends you back, you end up at the time they determine. Didn't you control your return?"

Tristan groaned at his mistake. "Yes, but I guess I forgot to focus on the time to come back to. I just concentrated on the place. Have I really been gone all day?"

"Try a week," Alastor commented, as he hurried into the room from the garden. "I knew you'd be okay."

Tristan caught the pointed look Alastor gave Mac and knew things hadn't exactly been cozy in his absence.

"I'm fine, Mac. I can take care of myself."

"That's not the point. You promised you wouldn't go down there without Alastor."

Tristan stepped out of Mac's embrace. "It was necessary, and as you can see, I'm perfectly fine."

"That's not the point. You promised."

"I told Alastor where I was going and he gave me directions so I wouldn't get lost. You have to trust I can take care of myself. Please, Mac."

Mac sighed and gave a reluctant nod. "Okay. But I still don't like it."

"You don't have to like it, you just have to trust me. Besides, it's not as if we don't worry when you're called up by the archangels. We all know they have the power to take you from us if they choose to do so."

Mac didn't argue the point and it seemed the discussion was over.

"What did you find out?" Alastor asked. "Did you speak to Lawrence?"

"I spoke with him, though I'm not sure I found out anything useful. He kept some of the memories of my past lives to use for bargaining. He used them to get better quarters down there and has no idea where they are now."

"I think we can safely say they're with whoever is messing with Tristan's dreams." Mac replied.

"And what do you think we should do about it?" Tristan asked.

"I don't see there's anything we can do except let the dreams run their course."

"Do you know where they're going to end up?"

"I have an idea," Mac admitted. "I just hope I'm wrong."

"What idea?" Alastor asked, but Mac would not be drawn further.

Chapter Twelve

Alastor didn't relish the idea of facing his old master, but he was becoming increasingly worried about Tristan's dreams and hoped the older demon might have some answers for him.

"Do you know who I am?" Alastor asked the haggard-looking demon.

"You were one of my demons until I fell."

"Yes. Do you know who I was before?"

"You were a human consigned to Hell for your crimes."

He had always known as much. "What do you know of my human lives?"

Aka Manah studied him. "I recruited far too many to my ranks to remember each individual."

"You remember nothing of me at all?"

Aka Manah beckoned him closer. "I remember you begging to keep a particular memory."

"I remember begging."

"I know. I recall your weakness that day and I still retain the memory you wanted to keep."

"You still have my memories?"

"I kept that one alone. I didn't want it finding its way back to you. The rest I've traded away over the centuries."

"To who?"

"To whoever wanted them at the time. I gave up many memories from many demons in order for a break in my torture until the end of the next century."

"Then you don't retain any memories from my past lives?"

"No, they're gone, save the one you once wanted so badly. It may interest you to know the last of your memories were traded quite recently, to a dream demon who was quite specific about what he wanted."

"Which dream demon?"

"One who merely acquired them for a superior, unless I'm very much mistaken. His master would not deign to lower himself to these levels of the pit just to collect a few memories."

"Do you know who he was—or who his master is?"

"The demon was a stranger to me, although his ultimate master—the leader of the dream demons—is known to me."

"You said he was specific about the memories he wanted. What did you mean?"

"He requested the ones featuring your current lovers."

"Do you know how the memories are being used against Tristan?"

"I've heard rumors. Even way down here an angel taking two demons into his bed is gossip-worthy. Tell me Alastor, has your own sleep been untroubled?"

"I've not had any nightmares like the ones Tristan has been suffering from."

"Perhaps he simply hasn't got to you yet."

"How do you know all this?"

"I might be imprisoned down here, but I keep my eyes and ears open. I may have been defeated, but I wasn't killed. I intend to escape the Underworld eventually, and when I do, I'll remember those who remained loyal to me, as well as those who weren't."

Alastor tried to ignore the implications of his former master's comment. "Do you know about the mortal prisoner of the Demon King?"

"Everyone knows of the Demon King's pet human." Aka Manah appeared surprised at the change of subject.

"Do you know if any dream demon has been in his company?"

"If he has, then it's been during the pet's dreams."

Alastor stood up to leave, but his former master's voice halted his step. "Don't you want to ask for the memory you wanted back?"

"Why would you want me to have it?"

"Maybe because now I want something in return."

"Such as?"

"My freedom."

"That isn't mine to give. I can't even figure out a way to get Cody released, and he's a far less important prisoner than you."

"You overestimate my value or underestimate his."

"Either way, I cannot free you."

"The memory you wanted above all others, in exchange for my liberty."

Alastor wished briefly he could help, before he chided himself for his selfishness. He was supposed to be figuring out a way to fix things, not create more problems.

"Maybe you think you'll have better luck persuading Nybbas to rein in whichever demon is disturbing your lover's slumber," Aka Manah suggested. "I hear he can be bribed for the right price."

"Nybbas?"

"The leader of the dream demons," Aka Manah explained. "He may have the answers you seek."

Alastor guessed his next step would be tracking down Nybbas.

* * * *

Alastor didn't bother going back to his lovers to report on what he had discovered. Deciding there was no time like the present, he set out down the tunnel leading to Nybbas, hoping to find some answers at last. From what his former master had told him, it appeared the leader of the dream demons might be approachable for the right price. Alastor wondered how much it would cost him to end this. He hoped the price wasn't too high.

He found Nybbas deep in the Underworld, his cavern home far more luxurious than any of the hovels he had previously seen, and certainly a big step up from the catacombs. Someone had scattered soft pillows around the cavern, and the flames in the sconces gave the place a romantic aura that seemed entirely out of place in the bowels of Hell.

Nybbas reclined on a comfortable looking chaise. He appeared contented and rather pleased with himself. His dark skin was covered in elaborate swirling golden tattoos and his horns were pure white, a strange contrast that was as unusual in the Underworld as Tristan's coloring.

"Alastor," he greeted him, waving him toward one of the other cushions. "To what do I owe the pleasure?"

Alastor sat, sinking into the overly soft cushions. "Thank you for seeing me," he offered, giving a nod of respect to the older and more powerful demon.

Nybbas smiled. "Think nothing of it. Please, have something to eat."

Alastor reached out to take a piece of fruit before remembering where he was. "Er…"

With a soft chuckle, Nybbas urged him to continue. "I don't seek to poison you or trap you here. I would recommend the grapes."

Alastor wasn't sure whether he believed Nybbas, but his host would certainly take it as an insult if he were to refuse his hospitality. Deciding to risk it, he popped a purple grape into his mouth.

"Now, what can I do for you?" Nybbas asked. "I take it this isn't a social call."

"No." Alastor shook his head. "I'm here to make a request of you."

"What sort of request would that be?" Nybbas asked.

Alastor gave him a tight smile. "My lover is suffering from unpleasant dreams, and we believe he's being shown parts of a past life. I believe a dream demon could be behind his torment."

"Perhaps his memories are merely surfacing now he's one of our ilk."

Alastor frowned. "How did you know I referred to Tristan?" he asked. "I have another lover."

Nybbas shrugged. "I don't believe Machidiel would let a few unpleasant memories bother him so much."

"You dare to speak Mac's name here in the Underworld," Alastor commented. "Most demons wouldn't have the nerve."

"Most demons are ridiculously superstitious," Nybbas countered. "Our present master encouraging such nonsense is to blame for that. I don't believe the ground will open up and swallow me if I dare to speak the name of an angel down here. Machidiel doesn't seem such a bad sort. His dreams are quite pleasant to see."

"You've seen Mac's dreams?"

"I have."

"When? Why?"

"Why not? I was curious to hear about the angel who had taken not one, but two demons into his bed. I wanted to see whether he really cared for you, or whether it was all a ploy to trap and destroy you."

"Mac wouldn't do that. He loves us."

Nybbas smiled as he continued to pick at the grapes. "I agree. I was most surprised to see his dreams."

Alastor realized the conversation had drifted and he attempted to steer it back on track. "Is there anything you can do to help Tristan?" he asked.

"I'm afraid not."

Alastor clenched his fists. "Just like that."

"I give my demons free rein to feed from who they choose and if they wish to have a little fun in the process, who am I to stop them?"

"Tristan isn't a mortal anymore. He's a demon like us."

"It makes no difference. Many of my demons feed only from the minds of other demons. It is a matter of personal preference. If one wishes to feed from Tristan, it is his or her choice."

A surge of frustration made Alastor feel sick with helplessness.

"Perhaps your angel can help him?" Nybbas suggested. "He has resources a demon does not."

"Mac has already tried to obtain the assistance of the archangels. They refuse to help."

"Are you sure?" Nybbas turned to the wall behind him and waved his hand once. The surface shimmered for a moment and Alastor watched as his own bedroom appeared. In the bed, Mac and Tristan had curled up together and, for the first time in many nights, Tristan appeared to be sleeping peacefully.

"He seems to be quite content," Nybbas commented. "Sleeping as soundly as a new born babe."

"He doesn't normally sleep this well," Alastor replied. "Not since the dreams started."

"Perhaps they are simply bad dreams?"

"No. They're memories of his past life."

Nybbas continued to watch the demon and angel on the wall. "Well, whatever they are, they aren't troubling him right now. It seems the presence of the angel comforts him."

Alastor shifted uncomfortably as he watched his lovers sleep peacefully without him.

"Is that a hint of jealousy I'm detecting?" Nybbas asked. "I thought the three of you were quite content with your relationship."

"We are!"

Nybbas lifted an eyebrow at Alastor's raised voice. "But perhaps you see they can be equally contented alone."

"We're a ménage," Alastor stated. "The three of us together."

Nybbas chuckled. "I'm well aware of what a ménage entails, but I'm not sure the three of you are truly meant to stay together in one."

"What's that supposed to mean?"

Nybbas watched him, yet declined to answer his question.

Alastor turned back to the wall and saw Tristan had woken up. His demon lover stretched and yawned. Mac opened his eyes and smiled.

"Sleep well?" the angel asked.

"Wonderfully," Tristan replied with a grin. "Perhaps Alastor has put a stop to my nightmares."

Mac sat up and looked around the room. "He doesn't appear to be back yet."

Tristan climbed onto Mac's lap and wriggled his arse. "I'm feeling a little hungry."

Mac groaned and fell back onto the mattress. "You're insatiable," he teased.

"I'm an incubus," Tristan reminded him. "And right now I want your arse."

Alastor watched as Mac spread his legs wider so Tristan could position himself between his thighs, ready to take what he needed from him. He wanted to be with them, not just watching, yet right now he couldn't see where he would fit. They didn't need him with them.

"You don't like to watch your lovers?" Nybbas asked. "They are quite beautiful to see, yet you don't seem to be enjoying the view."

"I would rather be with them."

Nybbas waved his hand and the images on the wall vanished. "You are jealous of what they have together. You can see, as can I, that they have no real need of a third in their relationship. Their souls are bound to each other."

"Soulmates," Alastor agreed.

"But where does that leave you?" Nybbas asked.

Alastor didn't know, nor did he want to. "Can you help with Tristan's dreams or not?" he snapped.

Nybbas seemed to take the hint that the pleasantries were over. "I cannot."

"When will they end?" Despite Tristan's pleasant nap in his absence, Alastor did not believe for a moment their troubles had vanished.

Nybbas stood and walked over to the entrance of the cavern. Alastor could tell their meeting was over and he joined him. "They end when I say so," Nybbas answered calmly.

Alastor thought for a moment he had misheard. "What?"

"I'm the one controlling Tristan's dreams."

"But why?"

Nybbas snapped his fingers and a blinding light flashed through the cave. When Alastor's eyes readjusted to the light, he saw Nybbas had summoned company. Cody sat in the middle of the cushions Alastor had previously occupied.

"Pleasant dreams, Alastor," Nybbas said before strolling over to Cody and pulling him into his arms.

Alastor had his answers, though not the ones he wanted. He took himself back to the apartment to report his findings to his lovers. He had a feeling his own nights were about to be disturbed and he was not looking forward to it at all.

* * * *

Tristan pounced on Alastor the moment he returned. "What did you find out? Do you know who might be screwing with my head at night?"

Alastor steered Tristan over to the sofa and flopped down on it with him.

"Was it a dead end?" Tristan asked. The disappointment was evident in his tone and downcast expression.

"Not exactly," Alastor admitted. "Where's Mac?"

"I'm right here." Mac joined them from the kitchen. "You don't look like a man with good news."

Alastor laughed without humor. "I'm not."

"Your former master couldn't help us?"

"He gave me a good lead, the perfect one in fact."

"Well, that's good, isn't it?" Tristan queried.

Alastor sighed. "I wish it was. Nybbas, the leader of the dream demons, is the one behind all this."

"But why?" Tristan asked. "I've never even heard of him."

"He's doing it for Cody," Alastor explained. "I saw them together as I left. Nybbas didn't say so outright, but he made it pretty obvious the two of them are lovers."

"And he won't help?"

"He let me waste my time with the enquiries, playing me for his own amusement, and then summoned Cody to make it clear where his loyalties lie."

"Did he give any indication how long this is going to go on for?" Tristan asked.

"I'm sorry. If anything, I think he's going to be playing in my mind as well."

"What makes you think so?" Mac asked. "Until now he's only targeted Tristan."

"I spoke with Aka Manah, my former master, before speaking with Nybbas. He gave some of the memories of my life to a dream demon, one who I guess works for Nybbas. Which means he probably intends to use them against me as well."

"At least he can't get any of Mac's memories," Tristan said. "It'll just be us two who never have a decent night's sleep again."

"If he chose to, Nybbas could tamper with my memories too," Mac informed them. "As leader of the dream demons, he has the power to do so."

The thoughts weren't pleasant ones and Alastor didn't want to admit out loud that the idea of going to sleep frightened him.

* * * *

Alastor knew he dreamt, yet the dream was like none he'd ever had before. He looked around the village, which appeared to be ancient. Bronze Age? Iron Age? He wasn't sure, though it definitely dated to before his time as a demon had begun. Despite the strangeness of his surroundings, there was a familiarity which made him realize he was probably seeing something from one of his past lives. As he had no memory of his mortal life and time moved differently in the Underworld, it was difficult for him to place exactly when he had walked the Earth as a man, though it wasn't a great stretch of the imagination to believe it might have been as long ago as the Bronze Age. Mac had been about an equally long time, having witnessed the exodus from Egypt with his own eyes.

People hurried around the village as though preparing for something. From the dark clouds gathering overhead he thought perhaps they hurried to finish their jobs before the storm hit. Alastor drifted toward the building which seemed to be the focal point of the activity. As long as he dreamt, he saw no harm in exploring as he wished.

"Brynn, come here," a voice he didn't recognize called from the doorway to the long hut.

Alastor took a step forward, wondering even as he did why he moved to answer to a name that wasn't his own. Then he realized something even stranger. He could understand the man, even though he could tell he wasn't speaking English. As a demon he had traveled widely and picked up many languages, yet he didn't recognize this one. Was it one he had forgotten?

He had returned to Earth as a demon in the time of the Ancient Greeks, and even though he had no recollection of having been on Earth before, he knew he must have been alive there at some point before that time.

"Brynn, now."

The older man waved in his direction and Alastor gazed about to see whose attention he tried to get. No one stood near him and he realized the man called to him.

"Where's your sister?" the old man asked, his voice gruff.

Alastor shrugged.

"Go find her."

Alastor turned away, wondering where to start searching for a girl he had never before set eyes on. He hoped the dream would give him the answer.

The rain came down in a steady drizzle as Alastor walked through the cluster of huts. He didn't mind the rain so much, though the strange clothes and footwear he wore seemed to soak up the water like a sponge.

They were approaching from the west when Alastor saw them. The clouds that seemed to linger over the village were localized and in the distance the sun had just started to dip below the horizon. The last rays of sunlight cast a golden glow over the two blond-haired men.

Mac and Tristan.

Alastor quickened his pace, his wandering sister forgotten, as he headed out to greet his lovers.

Mac and Tristan held hands, yet as he approached, they drew apart, creating a respectable distance between them. Obviously they hadn't recognized him yet.

"Mac, Tristan," he called, running across the muddy field toward them. They didn't look up as he called their names.

They did acknowledge him when he reached them, but no recognition shone on their faces. It was as if they were meeting a stranger.

"Mac?" Alastor reached out to pull Mac into a hug, but he stepped out of his way before he could touch him.

"Mac, what's the matter?" Alastor asked. "Aren't you glad to see me? What about you Tristan?"

Tristan stared at Mac in confusion before turning back to Alastor. "I think you've mistaken us for someone else." His voice was the same, but again the language sounded unfamiliar. It wasn't quite the same as the old man had spoken, but it was close enough for him to spot the similarities.

"Tristan, don't you remember me?" Alastor suddenly realized he spoke in a language other than English as well, though he had no idea what tongue he spoke. He recalled Tristan reporting similar oddities after his own troubled sleep. Alastor smiled to himself as he thought of protecting Tristan from whatever haunted him at night.

"You mistake me for someone else," Tristan said. "My name is Duach and this is Leith."

Alastor decided to go along with Tristan without argument. "I'm sorry. I guess you just remind me of people I knew. I'm Alastor."

Tristan smiled and gave a small nod.

"It's getting dark," Alastor commented as he turned round to walk back toward the village with them. "Do you have anywhere to stay tonight?"

Mac shook his head. "We would seek shelter in your village for the night if we may."

Alastor brightened considerably. As dreams went, it had started a little strange, yet now it took a familiar turn. Darkness falling, his lovers arriving, searching for shelter, *welcoming them to his bed. "I'm sure we can accommodate you." He smiled at each of his lovers as he led the way.*

Alastor knew he still dreamt, and he realized he was probably seeing something of his past life, but this wasn't so bad. Of course it would be better if Tristan and Mac knew him, but at least his dreams or memories were relatively pleasant compared to Tristan's nightmares.

From the corner of his eye he saw Mac and Tristan murmuring to each other, shutting him out and watching him with suspicion in their eyes.

"There's no need to be afraid of me," Alastor assured them.

"We're not afraid," Mac replied. "We're just having a rough time at the moment."

Suddenly Tristan fell to the ground and Alastor saw the back of his tunic was soaked in dark red blood. Alastor screamed at the sight of his lover in so much pain.

"Alastor, wake up!"

Alastor opened his eyes and blinked at Mac. "Mac?"

Mac pulled him into his arms and held him tight. "It's okay, sweetheart."

Alastor frowned. "Sweetheart?"

Mac's chuckle rumbled in his chest. "You think you have the monopoly on cutesy names? You call me angel and Tristan baby. Why can't I call you sweetheart?"

"Because I'm a bloody demon."

"So? You're still my sweetheart, whether you like it or not."

Alastor muttered something incoherent and burrowed closer into Mac's arms.

"Go back to sleep," Mac whispered. "I'm right here. I've got you."

"Looks like it's my turn for the bad dreams."

"Try to go back to sleep," Mac advised.

"I usually like dreaming about you and Tristan," Alastor murmured as he closed his eyes. "They're normally my favorite dreams."

Mac nudged his hips forward so their erections brushed together lightly under the sheets. "Mine too," he teased, kissing Alastor on the forehead. "Sleep now. We'll talk in the morning when Tristan's awake."

Mac expected Alastor to say something more, but he had already fallen asleep again.

* * * *

Alastor woke the next morning feeling irritable and tired. When he had gone back to sleep, he had once again seen Mac and Tristan in his dreams. They were clearly together in a relationship and he remained stuck on the outside, watching them. Even though the rational part of his mind told him they were all in a relationship together in the present day, he couldn't seem to squash his jealousy into submission.

"Coffee?" Mac asked, as he held out a mug each to Alastor and Tristan.

Alastor took his drink with shaky hands and blew on the liquid. Tristan, who seemed to have a stronger tolerance for scalding hot drinks, gulped his down like the coffee might evaporate if he left it in the mug for more than a minute.

"Bad night?" Alastor asked Tristan.

Tristan rubbed his eyes. "I seem to be scared all the time in my dreams. It's like I can never be completely at ease. There's always someone watching me and I live in fear they'll hurt me."

Alastor put his mug down on the bedside table and scooted back over to Tristan. "We won't let anyone hurt you. Just remember, it's all in the past. These things can't hurt us in the real world."

Mac sat at the foot of the bed with his own morning intake of caffeine. "You should probably take your own advice," he said quietly. "Do you want to tell us what plagued your dreams last night?"

As unsettled as the dreams made him, Alastor didn't think they were anywhere near as bad as the ones Tristan had been forced to have. "They're nothing to worry about." He brushed his own concerns aside.

"That's not what I asked," Mac pointed out. "When you woke in the night, you said you dreamed about the three of us, so why was your sleep troubled?"

"It's nothing," Alastor repeated. "It was just a bit disturbing, that's all."

Mac glared at him until he broke. "Fine, I dreamt about the two of you and from how Tristan has described his dreams, I'm pretty sure they were memories of the past as well."

Tristan twisted in Alastor's arms. "Why didn't you say something? How long have you been having these dreams?"

"Just last night," Alastor assured him.

Mac took another sip of coffee before he spoke. "At least we know Nybbas is definitely behind them."

"Mine aren't worth worrying about," Alastor assured his lovers.

"How about you let us decide that?" Tristan said.

"It's like I said to you, they're just dreams. They can't hurt us. And sooner or later Nybbas will become bored with tormenting us and we'll forget all about them."

"You forget he's no doubt doing this for Cody," Tristan reminded him. "We have a responsibility to get Cody out of the Underworld, and I don't think the dreams will stop until we do."

"If Nybbas is so concerned about Cody being a prisoner, why doesn't he rescue him personally?" Mac asked. "Surely he's in a better position to free him than any of us."

Alastor suspected the simple answer to that question was because Nybbas wasn't powerful enough to take on the Demon King. If Cody had been the prisoner of any other demon, he might have been able to free him, but the Demon King hadn't remained on his throne for this long by being weak.

"It's all about power," Alastor replied. "Nybbas hasn't the power to take on the Demon King. No one has."

Mac climbed off the bed and began to dress. "I'm going to speak with the archangels again. Maybe they know something more about Nybbas."

Chapter Thirteen

Mac left his lovers to go and speak with Michael. He knew Raphael should be his first port of call, but he was well aware of the fact he was starting to annoy his superior with his constant stream of questions and problems surrounding his demon lovers. He would take Michael up on his suggestion of approaching him for advice instead.

He found Michael in the training grounds, helping new angels become accustomed to their wings. Mac still recalled how long it had taken him to learn how to use them. It was like suddenly having a couple of extra limbs and his brain needed to be retrained to figure out how to operate them.

He hovered on the edge of the soft, cushiony ground and waited for Michael to approach him.

"What can I do for you?" Michael asked, as he reached Mac's side.

"I wanted to ask your advice about the demon, Nybbas."

"Nybbas, the leader of the dream demons?"

"Yes."

"You have reason to believe he's the one tormenting Tristan?"

Mac confirmed he had. "Alastor visited him yesterday in the Underworld. He saw Cody with him and now his dreams are also being disturbed. Nybbas made it clear he was behind the dreams—and doing this for Cody."

"It would seem that way."

"How powerful is Nybbas?"

"He's the most powerful of the dream demons, though they are not particularly high ranked in the grand scheme of things. Demons who can manipulate the physical world are higher up in the pecking order. Though manipulating a mind has its own degree of skill."

"Would he be powerful enough to take on the Demon King, if he chose to do so?"

"Not successfully, though he wouldn't be the first demon to have hidden talents the rest of the world isn't aware of." Michael gave Mac a small smile before continuing. "Your Tristan, for example, is far more powerful than most people give him credit for."

"He is?"

"Yes. Despite being an incubus, one of the lowest ranking demons, he is more powerful than Alastor and Lawrence combined."

Mac didn't know what to say. He had never imagined Tristan might be so powerful. The thought hadn't even occurred to him.

"But we've strayed from the subject," Michael said. "Nybbas. If what you're asking is whether he might be powerful enough to take on one such as the Demon King, then no, he isn't. It would be a suicide mission to even try."

"Then how are we expected to rescue Cody?"

Michael smiled and started to walk back onto the field. "I'm sure you'll find a way. Just remember, there's strength in numbers, and choose both your enemies and allies wisely."

Mac sighed with barely concealed frustration. He knew the archangels had a policy not to interfere too much, and to simply guide, but was it too much to ask for a few hints on what he should do?

* * * *

He was dreaming again, yet Alastor could still feel the aching of his arse from the pounding Tristan had given before he'd collapsed onto the mattress and fallen swiftly asleep.

It was night in his dream, which seemed strange since it had been morning when he'd fallen asleep. He slept in a pile of furs in a hut smelling of animals and earth. Sounds of snoring came from nearby and he turned to see if the man making the noise was close enough for him to prod in the back to get him to turn over.

He couldn't make out who the snorer was and as he peered around the room he forgot all about everything except Mac and Tristan and what they were doing in the quiet darkness of the hut.

Alastor watched as the two men moved slowly beneath the furs. They were so subtle about it, so quiet and careful in their movements. Alastor, who had woken to them making love so many times before, could recognize what they did in the darkness. Tristan was on his side with Mac spooning him. They were pressed together front to back, rocking slowly in the intimate dance. Alastor's breath hitched as he watched Tristan bite down onto his fist in an effort to stifle the sound of his groan. Alastor wasn't sure, but he thought he could see a dark trail of blood dripping from Mac's lip, where he had bitten it right through to keep from crying out loud.

His lovers were beautiful to watch together and Alastor moaned softly as his own body reacted to the visual stimulation. He wanted to go and join them across the hut, yet he knew if he moved toward them, they would stop and pretend to sleep until he returned to his own place. All he could do is watch them as they came together in quiet passion.

He reached beneath the furs and took himself in hand, matching their rhythm as best he could from across the room. The sight of his two men making love aroused him and he had to stifle his own groan as he spilled over his fingers.

After his lovers were done, curled together under the furs, Alastor finally closed his eyes and willed himself to wake up so he could lie with his lovers in their own bed, rather than watching them from across the room.

* * * *

Alastor climbed out of bed and wandered naked into the living room. He wasn't surprised to see his lovers had woken and followed him from the bedroom.

"Another dream?" Tristan asked as he buttoned up his jeans and took a seat.

"Yes."

"It seemed a bit more pleasant than the others," Tristan suggested with a teasing smile.

"Did you dream of us?" Mac asked.

Tristan chuckled and swung his legs onto the sofa so he sat stretched out facing Alastor. "Of course he did. Or didn't you notice the wet patch on the sheets from where he came?"

Alastor blushed. He hadn't realized anyone had noticed he'd had a wet dream, the first one he could recall having in centuries.

Tristan reached out a foot to rub against Alastor's leg. "I just want to know which of us he dreamt he was shagging and whether it was good."

"Neither, actually," Alastor replied loftily.

"Are you cheating on us with a dream guy?" Tristan teased, as he tormented Alastor by stroking his inner thigh. "Is there someone tall, dark, and handsome coming to you in your dreams?"

Alastor stilled Tristan's wandering foot with his hand. "The men in my dreams are blond." He tickled Tristan's sole. Tristan laughed as he tried to pull away. Alastor didn't let him escape, though he stopped tormenting him and instead placed the appendage back where it had been. "I dreamt of watching the two of you make love."

Tristan drew in a sharp breath. "Didn't you join us?"

Alastor studied his hands rather than meet his lover's gaze. "In my dreams, you two are together and have no need of me."

Tristan inched closer and forced Alastor to face him again. "If your dreams really are memories too, then it's just a matter of time before we are three again. I could never resist you for long."

"Do you think so?" Alastor asked hesitantly.

"It's possible we all loved each other in a past life," Mac contemplated. "Many people believe soulmates find each other again and again each time they're reincarnated."

"Most people who believe in soulmates believe it is two people, usually a man and a woman."

"I don't care what most people think. I believe the three of us are only complete when we're together. If we did live another life together, I don't remember it."

Tristan twisted round to face Mac. "I thought you remembered your mortal life?"

"I do remember it. I just don't remember the one you and Alastor seem to be dreaming about. A mortal may live many lives before they take their place in Heaven. I remember my last life and I don't recall either of you being in it. It's entirely possible I lived many lives between the one you two are dreaming about and my last life before becoming an angel.

Alastor wished he could remember his mortal life. The dream, as arousing as it had been, still disturbed him. Why would someone show him sex dreams while torturing Tristan with nightmares? He had a horrible feeling these dreams were just the start of his torment. He knew his past to be a dark one, even if he couldn't recall the details. He'd gone to Hell after he died. He hadn't been a good man during his last life. He'd done at least one purely evil deed, and deep down he suspected he knew what it was.

Murder.

He shivered and wished he'd dressed before coming out of the bedroom. Suddenly the dreams — memories — took on another aspect. What if he had known Mac and Tristan in his *last* life? What if they had been lovers then, too? He knew he would die to protect either one of them. Would he kill to protect them, too? Was his love for these two men the reason he had gone to Hell?

* * * *

Alastor saw them slip away into the trees shortly before the evening meal. He ignored his sister's call and followed them along what passed for a path through the woods.

"I think he knows," Tristan said to Mac, as Alastor approached them as stealthily as he could manage on the dry leaves and twigs littering the ground.

"You're imagining things. I'll admit he's a little strange, but all he's done is watch us a little more closely than everyone else."

"What if someone's told him about us? What if he knows about what we do with each other? What if we're driven out of this village, too?"

"We walked for many days and nights before we reached here. It's farther away than anyone we know has traveled before. Who could have told him what happened?"

"I don't know, but I'm telling you he knows. I see the way he watches you. It's like he's waiting for his chance to get you alone. What if he hurts you?"

"It's just your imagination. Now, since we're alone…"

Mac dipped his head to press his lips to Tristan's. Somehow Alastor knew they had been talking about him. Other than the dream he had had of watching them during the night, he had no recollection of what had happened since they had entered the village. It seemed, however, they had settled in there and planned to make it their home. He hoped they did, because he wanted both men more than he'd ever wanted anything in his life.

The memory of what they had together in the present conflicted with the knowledge he had yet to experience intimacy with either man in the past. It was confusing and frustrating.

Even more worrying was the way Tristan spoke to Mac as though he had no idea who Alastor was. Tristan had dreamed of the past too, so why didn't he recognize Alastor now?

Tristan made a high keening noise as Mac pushed him up against an oak tree and tugged at their clothes.

"We should be careful," Tristan gasped in a last ditch plea for caution which came far too late.

They came together with grunts and cries. Alastor's arousal became increasingly painful as the two lovers reached their climax. He had to have them.

Alastor woke with a startled cry and a sore neck. He hadn't meant to fall asleep again, and not on the sofa. Why was he so tired these days?

"Coffee?" Tristan asked as he handed him a mug.

Alastor took a welcome sip. "Thanks. Did you sleep as well?"

Tristan nodded. "You dreamt about the past again?"

"Yeah. We were all there again, though you still didn't know me. It's like the you in my dream has no memory of what's happening here and now."

"It's the same for me." Tristan sat on the sofa. "I know who I am and the role I'm supposed to be playing in the past, yet you and Mac seem to be really there. Nothing I say or do seems to make any difference to the outcome of the dreams. Which I suppose makes sense if they're really memories. In my dreams, you scare me."

"Why?"

"I don't know. It's like I know something bad is going to happen, but I don't know what. I think you're a part of it though."

Alastor sighed. "If there's going to be trouble, I guess I'm usually right in the middle of it."

Tristan chuckled. "Oh I think I could give you a run for your money there."

"Good thing we have Mac to keep us out of mischief, isn't it?"

Tristan snuggled up to Alastor and sighed contentedly. "What do you think will happen in the dreams?"

"I don't know."

"But you have an idea."

"Yes."

"Just like Mac has an inkling he won't elaborate on."

Alastor gave his own sigh, but it was far from contented. "I think you know where they'll end too, if you give it a bit of thought."

"I have thought about it."

"And?"

"And we'll end up dead, won't we?"

"I think so."

"I'm guessing it won't be us dying of old age, warm in our bed, will it?" Tristan gazed at Alastor with hope in his eyes. Alastor smiled sadly. He wouldn't put money on that outcome, no matter how much he liked the idea.

* * * *

Alastor reclined in the hot tub, trying to relax and failing completely. The dreams were getting to him and he tormented himself over where they would end.

"What are you hiding out here for?" Tristan asked, as he leaned on the edge of the tub.

"I'm not hiding."

Tristan splashed water at him. "Looks like you are to me."

Alastor closed his eyes. There was no hiding anything from his lovers. They knew him far too well. "You can join me if you like."

Tristan quickly stripped off his clothes and climbed into the tub. "I have the feeling you didn't invite me to join you so we could have some sexy fun in the tub."

Alastor sighed and sank down a little farther into the water.

"When was the last time you had a good night's sleep?" Tristan asked. "I know you're still having the dreams, so don't try lying."

Alastor opened his eyes and held out his arms for Tristan to crawl into them. "Come here, baby."

Tristan didn't hesitate to climb onto his lap and they rubbed against each other for a few minutes, simply relishing the touch of flesh against flesh.

Alastor groaned as he gripped Tristan's buttocks beneath the water. "I get so jealous when I dream about you and Mac together."

Tristan nipped his ear. "Why would you feel that way when you have me right in your arms?"

"I can't help it. The dreams—memories—Nybbas feeds me at night are driving me crazy with desire."

"At least your dreams seem to be pleasant," Tristan pointed out. "I dream of being chased out of villages, beaten to a pulp, and ostracized from everyone, save for Mac."

"Pleasant?" Alastor replied sarcastically. "I wouldn't say that. He makes me watch the two of you together. Every night I watch Mac fuck you and neither of you look twice at me."

"Mac fucking me, huh?" Tristan asked. "Tell me about them. Tell me what you see in your dreams."

Alastor's cock filled at Tristan's breathy words.

"Tell me," Tristan begged. "Feel how hard it makes me."

Alastor could feel Tristan's arousal pressing against his belly. How could he refuse his lover's quiet plea?

"Last night I watched Mac take you in a stream. You knelt in the water, the top of your body on the grassy bank, while he fucked you from behind."

"Sounds hot," Tristan said. "I can almost feel him right here."

"He won't be home for a while yet."

"Guess your fingers will have to do for the moment then."

"What about my cock?"

Tristan laughed. "Later. You can't tell me about your dreams if you're coming."

"Tease."

"Yep. Now finger me hard while you tell me what else you dreamt about."

Alastor pushed two fingers straight into Tristan's arse and waited until he started to move before speaking again. "I see Mac take you against trees, on beds of heather, beneath the furs of your bed at night."

"Do I ever fuck him?" Tristan asked, as he rocked on Alastor's fingers.

"Not that I've seen," Alastor admitted. "Mac fucks you so thoroughly you wouldn't have the energy to take him, too."

"Maybe that's why I need you. I need to be the one in charge sometimes. I need to feel my cock sliding into another man's arse. Your arse, Alastor."

"It doesn't seem to me like you're missing topping a man all that much back then. You never even look twice at me, except to cast me a wary glance when you catch me watching you."

"Maybe you should just dive right in and spread your legs for me," Tristan suggested. "Show me what I'm missing."

Alastor wished things were so simple. "If only I could. When I'm dreaming I seem to just drift along without any real control over what's happening. Perhaps it's because they're memories and I have to see what actually happened."

"Maybe," Tristan agreed. "Nybbas seems to be playing on your insecurities and my fears."

"Why do you fear what people think about you? You've never really had to suffer from homophobic bullies or anything like that."

"I don't know. I wonder if perhaps this is the best ammunition Nybbas has from my memories to unsettle me. Showing me happy memories of how Mac loved me back then wouldn't have the same effect as it has on you."

"You're right about that," Alastor said. "I just hope this is the best Nybbas can throw at me."

"You're worried maybe it isn't?"

"Something tells me there's more for me to see, and I'm not going to like it."

"What makes you think so?"

"I'm not sure. Something Michael said about making sure we finish this before it plays out to the end. That—and a little gut instinct."

Tristan's expression clouded over. "You're probably right, but let's not worry about the future for now. Fuck me, Alastor."

"You haven't fed yet today," Alastor reminded him. "Perhaps you should top."

"I'll see if Mac will let me fuck him when he comes home."

"I *am* home," Mac announced from the doorway to the garden. "And you know you don't have to ask to feed from me."

"How are we going to do this?" Tristan asked. "Who first?"

Alastor tried not to think about how, if it were just Mac and Tristan, the question wouldn't be necessary.

"Tristan to feed from me first." Mac undressed and joined them in the hot tub. He rubbed his knuckles across Tristan's jaw. "You're looking peaky, love."

Tristan's eyes flashed a brighter red and he climbed off Alastor's lap, dislodging the fingers that had stilled in his arse. "Turn round," he ordered.

Mac turned onto his knees and gripped the edge of the tub. Alastor watched as Tristan scooted across and eased Mac's legs apart. His lovers didn't waste any time with preparation and Tristan took Mac swift and hard.

"Holy shit!" Mac cried, causing Alastor to chuckle.

"It must be good if you're using that expletive," Alastor explained, when Mac and Tristan turned to stare at him over their shoulders.

Mac opened his mouth to reply, but with Tristan pounding his arse, he appeared to be having difficulty in forming words. Having been in Mac's position more times than he could count, Alastor could understand his predicament.

"Don't just sit there." Tristan thrust inside Mac. "Get over here and join us."

Alastor inched over to them and sighed. "I can't fuck you from this angle."

"You can get your fingers in me," Tristan suggested. "Or you can climb out of the tub and feed Mac your cock. Let him suck you while I fuck him."

Mac shivered.

"I see you like the idea," Tristan said. "How about it, Alastor?"

Alastor didn't need any more encouragement—he climbed out of the tub and walked round to the other side. Mac licked his lips, ready to taste him. Alastor stroked his already hard length and stepped forward. Mac's lips were just out of reach of the head.

Tristan laughed. "Stop teasing him. Can't you see he's practically begging for your dick?"

"I can't hear him begging." Alastor brushed the tip of his penis across Mac's lips, giving him just the smallest of tastes.

"You want me to beg?" Mac gasped as his tongue chased Alastor's taste across his lips. "I'll beg if you want."

Alastor touched the tip of his erection to Mac's lips for just a second. "I want."

Mac cried out as Tristan increased his pace behind him. "Please, Alastor, please."

Since it was quite clear to Alastor that Mac was losing the power of speech at a rather rapid pace, he took pity on him and slid his cock into Mac's eager mouth.

The angle wasn't perfect and Alastor made a mental note to see about raising the level of ground around the tub so he could do this next time without straining.

Mac sucked him slowly.

Alastor pushed the fingers of one hand into Mac's hair, while keeping the other hand on the edge of the tub to retain his balance. "That's it," he groaned. "Suck me dry."

Mac hummed a response and Alastor nearly lost his footing entirely at the sensation.

Tristan was already well on his way to an orgasm. Alastor caught his eye and Tristan placed one of his hands over Alastor's on the edge of the tub.

"Don't think about the past," Tristan said. "This is what's important. Here and now, the three of us together. It doesn't matter what happened before, none of it does."

"You don't know that," Alastor argued.

Mac sucked on him harder in response, his way of saying to shut up and enjoy what they had right now. Alastor took his silent advice and closed his eyes. He could tell when Mac came a few minutes later, his mouth slackened around Alastor's penis and he slumped forward. Tristan had clearly done his job well.

"Are you close, Tristan?" Alastor asked.

Tristan howled a response the neighbors probably heard on the roof of the flats across the street. The sound went right through him and when Mac recovered himself enough to suck on his length again, he came so hard he thought he might just fly right off the roof and into the clouds.

He wasn't sure how he got back into the hot tub, but when he came to his senses again, he was leaning back against Mac, with Tristan resting in front of him.

Tristan spoke first. "*This* is what's important."

Alastor gripped him tightly about the chest. "I know, yet I can't help worrying about what else is coming in my dreams."

"They'll come no matter what, so why worry about them?"

Mac pressed his lips to the indent of Alastor's neck. "It isn't just the jealousy of seeing me and Tristan together, is it?"

"That's a big part of it," Alastor replied.

"But not all."

"No."

Tristan took his hands in his and squeezed them. "What else plagues you?"

"I just have a really bad feeling about all this. What would be the point of showing me all these memories of you two together? Sure, it makes me jealous and horny, but you two are right here with me when I wake up, so why bother? There has to be something more to this."

"What more could there be?"

Alastor kissed the top of Tristan's head. "I think the life I'm seeing is the last one I lived."

"What makes you think so?"

"Just a feeling, a kind of dread I can't shake, even when I wake."

"You appear the same in my dreams as you do now," Tristan commented. "Almost exactly the same. Maybe a little shorter, but that's it."

"Alastor has made himself taller over the years since becoming a demon," Mac whispered, as though he didn't like to mention the fact.

Alastor frowned as he tried to recall whether he had seen himself in his dreams. With no mirrors or any reflecting surface he hadn't had the opportunity. He tried to think what Mac and Tristan had looked like and realized there were slight differences in their appearances then to how they appeared now.

"Mac is much shorter in my dreams," Alastor said. "And Tristan, your hair was lighter, like you spent all day out in the sun and it bleached it. I think your nose might have been a little narrower and Mac's ears were a little bigger too. You were both recognizable, but there were definite differences to how you appear now."

"I've noticed the differences in Mac as well," Tristan admitted. "What do you think it means?"

Mac sighed. "It could mean you and I have lived other lives since the one the two of you are dreaming about. Our bodies, while remaining similar, are not quite the same as they were then. Alastor, if he is the same as you recall, could be dreaming about his last life. The only change in him, from what you're saying, is his height, and he's altered that himself since becoming a demon."

"Then I could be dreaming of the life I went to Hell for."

"I shouldn't have said anything." Tristan tried to twist round in Alastor's tight embrace.

"Why keep quiet about it?" Alastor asked. "It's not like I don't suspect this to be the case already."

"But I didn't have to confirm it for you. And maybe I'm wrong. Who remembers everything they dream about?"

"These aren't just dreams though, are they?" Alastor pointed out. "They're memories, and Nybbas wants us to remember them. Nybbas wants us to suffer, and this is his best way of doing it."

"Well, he's certainly putting the two of us through the ringer," Tristan muttered. "Though lucky old Mac sleeps easy at night."

"That's probably because he hasn't got to me yet," Mac pointed out.

"I don't want to remember any more," Alastor admitted. "If I'm right, I went to Hell at the end of this life. I don't want to know what I did to warrant that."

Alastor thought he felt the soft brush of lips on his neck before Mac spoke in his ear. "You know what you did. You've always known."

"I murdered an innocent," Alastor said. "I don't want to see it, though."

"I don't want you to either," Mac agreed. "But I don't see how you can avoid it. If Nybbas has that memory too, and there's no reason to suppose he doesn't, sooner or later, when he's finished tormenting the two of you, he'll force you to relive your crime."

Alastor drew in a sharp breath, trying to gather the courage to say what he needed to. "I'm scared, Mac."

"We all are," Tristan replied. "We just have to stick together and ride out the storm."

Alastor could feel Mac nodding. "We have to leave the past in the past and concentrate on the future."

"Easy for you to say," Alastor muttered. "You don't have blood on your hands."

"Of course I do. I killed in the war, just the same as the rest of the angels."

"That's different."

"A life is a life," Mac argued. "None is more or less valuable than another."

"A demon's life is worthless," Alastor said.

Mac hugged him, pulling Tristan nearer as well. "Not to me," he whispered. "Never worthless to me."

Chapter Fourteen

Mac stood at the archway which led to the chamber where the archangels congregated. He'd been here for hours and still he had yet to see a single one of their kind.

Angels glanced at him curiously as they passed him by and went about their business.

He wondered if he was wasting his time or whether one of the archangels might take pity on him and grant his request. It didn't make any difference whether they did or not. Their chamber held the pool that would show him what he wanted to see, and he'd sneak in to use it if he had to.

Mac thought back to the time, not so long ago, when Raphael had offered to let him see Alastor at his worst. Mac had refused, knowing he didn't want to see him commit the deed that had sealed his fate and sent him down to Hell when he died. He wished now he had taken Raphael up on his offer instead of practically throwing it back in his face. If Alastor was really remembering his final past life as a form of revenge, it was simply a matter of time before Nybbas made him relive the moment he committed murder. At least if Mac knew what had happened all those centuries ago, he could do his best to help him handle the impact the memory would have on him.

All he needed was Raphael or one of the other archangels to appear, so he could ask permission of them to see what had happened.

He wasn't sure how long he had paced in front of the chamber before Michael appeared in the archway. Mac bowed and greeted him with all the respect due to the archangel, maybe even a little more since he was, after all, going to beg a favor from him.

"Machidiel, what brings you back here again?" Michael's question was politely spoken.

"I seek permission to view Alastor's mortal past."

Michael led Mac away. "Let us walk."

Mac would have felt more hopeful had the walk not been away from the chamber that housed the pool of visions.

"You and Raphael are still at odds," Michael commented. There was no judgment in his tone. He merely made an observation. Mac couldn't deny the truth of his words.

They walked in silence until they reached the archway leading to the residences of the angels who, for various reasons, chose not to return to Earth at all. Michael led Mac over to a golden bench that was far more comfortable than the solid gold metal suggested. "You still resent the fact that Raphael wouldn't help you with Cody."

"Yes." Mac didn't deny it or try to keep the disapproval from his voice. "He's an innocent, trapped in the Underworld, and Raphael could have prevented it." Mac stopped himself from adding that Michael could have stepped in too.

"Everything happens for a reason."

"What reason could there possibly be for this?" Mac's temper bubbled just below the surface until Michael placed a calming hand on his arm.

"Cody will be fine. I promise. There will soon be a new Demon King and Cody's imprisonment will end with the new reign."

"I've not heard any rumors of a demon strong enough to take on the current monarch."

"No, you wouldn't have."

"Then how can you be so sure?"

Michael smiled. "The oracles have spoken of what is to come."

"The oracles aren't always right."

"No. And they may be wrong this time. I don't believe so though."

"Did Raphael know about their vision when he refused to help?" Somehow it was important he knew the answer to this.

"No, the oracles finished their report just minutes ago. It is why we have been secluded in the chambers for the better part of a day."

Mac strained to keep his anger in check. "Then he should have helped."

"He might not have known how things would play out, but he did know it wasn't his place to interfere. Cody's journey will not be an easy one. He is, however, right where he needs to be and on the path fate has chosen for him."

Michael's words were spoken with finality and signaled the end of the discussion. Mac hoped the archangel told him the truth.

"What of Alastor?" Mac asked quietly. "Raphael once asked me if I wished to see him at his worst."

Michael raised his hand to halt Mac's words. "You refused the offer."

"I know. I should have said yes."

"Seeing Alastor commit murder will do nothing to stop the dreams. He will still remember what he has done."

"But if I know what is to happen in his dreams, I can help him. I can warn him."

Michael shook his head. "You can best help him by being with him when he needs you."

"But—"

Michael stood up and looked down kindly at Mac. "He needs you with him. You should return to him now."

Michael didn't give him a choice in the matter. With a wave of his hand he sent Mac back to Earth and he knew he had lost his chance to see what Alastor's dreams would bring. All he could do is hope Alastor's past didn't destroy their future.

* * * *

A visit from Raphael, especially when he hadn't summoned him, could mean one thing alone— trouble. Mac wondered what could have happened to bring the archangel down to Earth.

Raphael turned to Alastor and Tristan. "Leave us."

Neither demon questioned the order. They scurried from the kitchen with worried glances at Mac.

"Go into the bedroom," Raphael called after them. "I'll not have them listening in on our discussions," he explained to Mac.

Mac remained silent.

"You're wondering why I'm here," Raphael said.

"Yes, of course."

"I heard a rumor you'd asked Michael to view Alastor's past life. Is it true?"

"Yes."

"I made the offer to you some time ago."

"I know."

"Why didn't you come to ask me this time?"

"You were not there."

"I'm your direct superior."

Mac cringed. "I meant no slight to you."

"Had you asked me, even then, I would have given my permission."

Mac couldn't have been more surprised if Raphael had suddenly announced his intention to take a demon as a lover of his own. Before he could ask if the offer was still open, Raphael spoke again.

"Unfortunately, Michael has now forbidden any archangel from allowing you access to the pool of visions."

"He can do that?"

"He can."

"I thought all archangels were equal."

"In most things we are, but occasionally Michael pulls rank on the rest of us, and this would appear to be such a time."

"Then there's no way I can see what Alastor did in his past life."

"There is one way."

Mac waited as patiently as he could for Raphael to elaborate.

"You were a part of Alastor's life and a witness to his crime," Raphael explained. "Your memories of what happened are all within your mind. You simply need to know how to access them."

"Would regression hypnosis work?"

"Maybe, but I think you'll find meditation on your own far more reliable."

"Why are you helping me with this?" Mac asked. "Aren't you going against the wishes of Michael in doing so?"

"Michael has forbidden you access to the pool of visions. Your memories are a different matter entirely."

"But they will show me the same thing."

"Mostly. The pool of visions will show you what happened as an observer, while your memories will place you within the events, though you'll have no more control over your actions whilst you're there than Tristan and Alastor have over their actions in their dreams."

"Why are you helping me when Michael wouldn't?"

"Because, unlike Michael, I believe you need to see what Alastor is capable of. Michael believes humans forget their past lives for a reason and to remember them can serve no purpose."

"I thought we all get to where we are because of our pasts. That we are the sum of our experiences, both the good and the bad."

Raphael sat at the table opposite Mac. "Humans learn from their past lives without ever having to remember them. It has always been this way. For the most part, there is no need for anyone to remember their past lives. In this situation however, I disagree. Tristan and Alastor are remembering the past and you need to, as well."

"I remember my last life completely."

"Yes, all angels recall their most recent life."

"But I don't remember Alastor or Tristan being in it."

"Tristan was there, but Alastor had already earned his place in Hell by that time."

Mac tried to recall Tristan, but as hard as he concentrated, he could not remember ever meeting his blond lover before. "Are you sure I knew Tristan in my last life?"

"Yes. He has been in many of your past lives, including your last."

Mac closed his eyes as he struggled to remember. "Did he appear as he does now?"

"Yes, though perhaps a little the worse for wear."

"Were we lovers?" If they had been and he still couldn't remember, then Mac wasn't sure what he would do.

"Not in your last life, though I suspect you might have been had Tristan lived a little longer."

"He died?"

"Despite your best efforts to save him."

Mac had always known he'd been a healer in his past life, and he sorted through the memories of those he had tried and failed to save all those centuries before. Suddenly, he saw him. His face had been almost unrecognizable following the attack of the wild boar. By the time Mac had reached him, he had already lost too much blood to be saved. Even in the modern world, Tristan's life would have been on the line with those injuries. In the past, with just the most primitive of implements, Mac had been unable to save Tristan. He didn't even know what his lover's name had been. They had not been lovers or even friends. Mac had been with him at the end of his life and had watched him pass on, much as he had done with many other men and women. He had mourned him as he had done each person he failed to save.

"I didn't even recognize him." Tears rolled down Mac's face.

"Your soul did," Raphael answered. "You and Tristan have always found each other. Your destinies are irrevocably entwined."

"What of Alastor's destiny?"

"His path has crossed that of your own and Tristan's just once. If you look far enough back into your past lives, you'll see him."

"Is his destiny to be with the two of us?"

"He's a demon."

"That isn't what I asked."

"I see the destiny of my angels, not of demons. Your destiny is clear to me, as is that of Tristan, because his destiny is so much a part of your own."

"Then you're saying Alastor's destiny isn't?"

Raphael shuffled his feet as he turned away from Mac. "I don't know. In your first life, you knew them both. In subsequent lives, you have known Tristan alone."

"Then Alastor is remembering my first life?"

"Yes. It was also his first and only life. His actions in it sent him to Hell. Had he made different choices, he might have lived many lives like yourself and Tristan. As it is, his life touched your own very briefly, at least until now."

Mac stood up and began to pace. "Do you believe he should be punished forever just because of his actions in one life?"

"He took the life of another."

"I know, you've told me so before. He doesn't even remember."

"Just because he doesn't recall his crime, it doesn't make it any less reprehensible."

"Everyone deserves a second chance."

"If you can save him then he'll have such a chance."

Mac ran his hands through his hair in frustration. "I don't know how. I know how to heal the body, not the soul."

Raphael reached across and patted Mac on the arm in a gesture of comfort. It had been so long since Raphael had sought to reassure him, Mac felt his eyes water. "As much as it pains me to admit it, you're already healing his soul."

"Why do you think that?"

"Because he suffers. His conscience troubles him more and more the longer he remains with the two of you. He shows remorse and feels guilt. Since entering this relationship with you and Tristan, he has not corrupted a single human, and he has been using his powers less frequently with each passing day."

"Can he be saved if he keeps on this path?"

"I don't know."

"Can I ask you why you hate Alastor so much?" Mac wondered if the word hate was the right one to use. Archangels weren't supposed to hate anyone—no angel should—yet Raphael seemed to truly despise Alastor. "And don't tell me it's because he's a demon. You don't seem to have the same passionate hatred for Tristan, and he is just as much a demon as Alastor now."

Raphael wouldn't meet his eyes. "Tristan is a demon through no fault of his own. Alastor is a demon because of his own actions. Take a look at his mortal life, Machidiel. Take a good, long look at your lover, and then you'll know why I hate him—yes, I admit I hate him, even though, as an archangel, I shouldn't. You may even find yourself agreeing with me."

"I could never hate Alastor."

Raphael began to fade away. "Never say never, Machidiel."

* * * *

Tristan watched as Mac and Alastor kissed in front of him. A part of him knew he was watching Leith and Brynn come together for the first time, while the rest of him was perfectly aware of the life they had shared together in the future.

Brynn kissed Leith with a desperation that told Tristan he had never found pleasure with another man before now. Leith was the one guiding him and taking control of the situation. Brynn let himself be carried away on a tide of lust.

Tristan wanted to join them, yet a part of him knew that hadn't happened in the past and wasn't going to happen now. He was an observer right now, not a participant. Brynn had taken Duach's place underneath Leith and Tristan watched as the two men writhed together on the bank of the stream. Instead of being jealous of Brynn being in his place, Tristan knew Duach had wondered what it might be like to be in Leith's place, to be the one in charge, the one sliding into another man's body.

Brynn's cries became louder and Tristan felt the first stirrings of unease. They were being careless. The village was too close and they were right here at the nearest source of water, where anyone might wander.

The sound of footsteps drew his attention away from the lovers. Turning to peer through the trees, he saw several men approaching with spears. A hunting party, who would soon see a different sort of quarry.

Tristan screamed as he woke. The last thing he had seen was the group of men appearing through the trees, spears at the ready.

Mac's arms were around him in an instant. "It's okay, love. You're safe now."

Tristan clung to his lover. "I want these nightmares to stop."

"I know."

"Something bad is going to happen," Tristan whispered. "Something worse."

"You just have to remember it's all in the past. It can't hurt you in the here and now."

Alastor stirred beside them and sat up. "Another dream?" he asked.

"Yes."

"Me too."

"What did you dream about?" Tristan asked, curious to know if they had been dreaming about the same event at the same time.

"I dreamt of Mac taking me," Alastor confirmed. "But all the time you stood there, calling him back to you, trying to split us up."

It wasn't the exact same scenario Tristan had dreamt of, but he had a feeling they were both being manipulated with regard to what they saw. He wondered briefly which version of events, if either, was the true one.

"Nybbas is cherry-picking which memories to show you," Mac said. "I suspect he's also altering things slightly to make whatever point he wants to."

Tristan agreed. "All I felt as I watched the two of you was desire. I didn't want to part the two of you. I felt then as I do now. The two of you coming together is a beautiful thing to see."

"We have to find a way to stop Nybbas," Mac declared. "The two of you can't go on like this."

"But how are we going to do that?" Tristan asked.

Mac didn't answer. Tristan suspected he had no more clue how to end their torment than he and Alastor did.

* * * *

Mac couldn't put it off any longer. Tristan and Alastor's nightmares were tearing them apart and Mac had to know how much worse they would become. Stretching out on the bed he closed his eyes and began to meditate. With so much on his mind, it wasn't exactly easy to relax enough to access the memories trapped in his head.

"What are you doing?" Mac's eyes opened and he saw Alastor standing at the side of the bed.

"Thinking." Mac closed his eyes again.

The bed dipped as Alastor sat on the edge. "You want some help with that," Alastor teased as he ran a finger down Mac's chest.

Mac batted Alastor's hand away. "Go check on Tristan."

"Tristan's fine. I'd rather stay and tease you."

Mac turned his head to glare at Alastor. He didn't need to say a word. Alastor backed off immediately and climbed off the bed. "Great, you just have yourself a nice little nap while the rest of us are trying to remember what a decent night's sleep actually is."

Alastor stamped his way over to the door. "Alastor, wait." Mac hadn't wanted to tell his lovers what he planned on doing, but he didn't want Alastor angry with him either. "Come back here and lie with me."

Alastor looked over his shoulder from the doorway.

"Please," Mac urged. "I'm sorry I snapped at you."

Mac patted the duvet, encouraging Alastor to stretch out beside him. Alastor curled up at his side like a contented cat, his arm wrapped around Mac's waist and his head on his shoulder. Mac wasn't sure having his lover draped across his body would help him concentrate, but he didn't have the heart to send him away again.

He could feel Alastor's heartbeat against his own and he could tell the moment his lover drifted off to sleep. Closing his own eyes again he tried to concentrate on the past.

Suddenly he saw a dark-skinned demon with white horns standing in front of him. "Need some help?" the demon asked.

Before Mac could reply, memories began to wash over him. Tristan was there, of course, smiling at him as they came together over and over again in one life after another. Farther and farther back Mac went, searching for his memories of Alastor.

Finally, so far back Mac couldn't even tell what century it was, he found his two lovers.

* * * *

"Duach." Alastor knelt beside Tristan. His back was to Mac and he didn't seem to know he was there. "I'm sorry. I didn't mean it."

"Mean what?" Mac asked.

Alastor spun round. "Leith!"

Mac saw the sharp instrument in Alastor's hand and the blood-red stain it bore. He rushed forward and shoved Alastor aside. "What did you do?" Alastor dropped his weapon and stared at Mac in mute horror. Tristan was bleeding badly, and Mac could tell he had been mortally wounded. "What happened?"

"Leith, I didn't mean it, I swear."

"Did you do this?" Mac asked.

"Yes, but –"

Mac picked up the weapon and turned it on Alastor. "Why?"

Alastor stared at Tristan, who was still clinging to life by the barest of threads. "He said you planned to leave."

"We are...were. The hunting party nearly caught us together. We were careless. It's simply a matter of time before our secret is discovered. We have to leave." Mac felt pretty sure Tristan wouldn't be going anywhere at all.

"Then you lied to me," Alastor growled. "Didn't what we shared mean anything to you?"

"Of course it did."

"Then why were you going to leave me?"

Mac threw aside the weapon. "We weren't. Duach and I had talked things through and we intended to ask you to come with us. We wanted to build a new life together, the three of us – away from those who would do us harm."

"Duach never mentioned that."

"Did you give him chance to before you decided to stab him?"

"I..." Alastor reached out, as though to touch Tristan.

"Get away from him," Mac shouted. "Go, and don't let me see your face again."

"Leith?"

Mac pulled Tristan into his arms and held him tightly. "Go now. If I see your face again, I'll kill you."

Alastor crept away through the trees and Mac tried to make Tristan as comfortable as he could. It was a hopeless task and a short time later, Tristan finally breathed his last.

Chapter Fifteen

Mac bolted from the bed, jostling Alastor awake. He ran for the bathroom and just reached the sink in time.

Alastor hurried after him and Mac shook off his hand as the demon tried to soothe him. "What is it, Mac?"

Mac ignored his question as he rinsed out his mouth with water.

"Mac, you're scaring me. What happened?"

Alastor reached for Mac's shoulder, but he pushed him aside. "You need to back off, right now," Mac warned.

"What's happened? Did you get one of these freaky dreams too?"

Mac pushed Alastor toward the door. "Just get out of here, Alastor, please."

Alastor seemed confused, and rightly so, but he left Mac alone in the bathroom with his thoughts, closing the door behind him.

"Raphael?" Mac called.

The archangel appeared immediately. "So, now you know."

"Alastor murdered Tristan."

"Yes. His jealousy and temper are a lethal combination."

"He doesn't remember what happened."

"If Nybbas isn't stopped, he soon will."

Mac sat on the edge of the bathtub. "It'll hit him badly when he finds out what he did."

"How are you handling the knowledge of what he did to earn his place in Hell?"

Mac wasn't sure he was coping very well at all. His stomach churned and he couldn't seem to forget the burning anger he felt for Alastor. Suddenly, he knew why humans forgot their past lives, for how could they move on if they remembered the intensity of such emotions? How could he be a good angel with such hatred tearing apart his soul?

"Come back with me." Raphael reached out his hand toward Mac. "Alastor is not worthy of your love, he never was."

"My assignment is to save him. How can I do so if I leave?"

"Do you still want to?"

Mac buried his face in his hands. He didn't know. "I need to talk to Tristan."

Raphael spread his wings. "I know you'll make the right choice."

Mac wasn't so sure. It seemed he hadn't made any good decisions since getting involved with Alastor.

Leaving the bathroom, Mac found Alastor in the bedroom, throwing his clothes into a suitcase in a haphazard manner. "What are you doing?" Mac asked.

"Getting my shit together." Alastor stooped to pick up a shirt from the floor. "I'll be gone within the hour and you won't see me again."

"What?" Mac was confused for just a moment. "You were eavesdropping."

"Of course. Would you expect anything less from a murderous demon?"

Mac stalked across the room and yanked Alastor away from the wardrobe. "Do you think you can get out of this so easily?"

"You think I'm going to find it easy to walk away?" Alastor shook Mac off him. "I love you and I'm going to lose you because of something I did hundreds of years ago—something I don't even remember."

"What's going on here?" Tristan asked from the doorway. "I could hear you yelling from the kitchen."

"I'm leaving," Alastor said. "I should never have come between the two of you in the first place. I have to plead ignorance since I don't recall what happened the last time I did so."

Mac cringed at the reminder Alastor didn't even know exactly what had happened in the past. Of course, he knew what he had overheard a short while before, but he didn't remember, not like Mac did.

"Mac, has something happened?" Tristan asked.

"I searched through my memories of the last life when the three of us knew each other."

"You mean the one me and Alastor have been dreaming about?"

"Yes. The memories of that life are still in my head, locked away for the most part, but accessible if I really want to see them."

"And what did you see?"

"I saw your death, by Alastor's hand."

Tristan stumbled toward the bed and sat down shakily. "Alastor killed me?"

"Apparently," Alastor muttered. "Now we all know who the bad guy is around here, I'll leave you to get on with your lives in peace."

"No."

Mac turned to his younger lover. "He killed you, Tristan."

"I heard you the first time," Tristan said. "But we still need to get Cody out of the Underworld, and I can't do it alone."

"Fine," Alastor agreed. "I'll stay to help with Cody then I'm out of here."

Tristan glanced uneasily at Mac. "Do you really want what we have between the three of us to end?"

Mac didn't know and couldn't bring himself to speak.

Alastor sat down beside Tristan, though he made no move to touch him. "You and Mac are destined to be together. I see that now. I should never have interfered—not then and not now."

Tristan reached for Alastor's hand and squeezed it. "I seem to recall I wanted you to interfere."

Alastor snatched his hand back. "We both know sooner or later we'll relive what Mac has already seen. Let's just cut our losses now before you hate me, too."

"I could never hate you," Tristan said.

"Never say never," Mac whispered, echoing the words of the archangel.

"See, Mac's an angel, and even he hates me for what I did to you."

Tristan nudged Mac, as though prompting him to deny the accusation. Mac didn't say a word. Tristan didn't understand, at least not yet. Once he had relived his death at the hands of their lover, he wouldn't be so quick to forgive.

"Let me go," Alastor begged.

"I see everyone's having fun here."

Mac turned toward the new speaker and saw Nybbas standing across from them, leaning against the wall.

"Not as much as you are," Alastor said. "You've won. You've destroyed us. Why are you here now – to gloat?"

"I didn't destroy you," Nybbas replied. "You managed that all on your own. I just opened your eyes to the truth. Had your relationship been as strong as you believed, it would have survived."

Tristan stood and glared at Nybbas. "Our relationship *will* survive this. The truth can only make it stronger."

"I don't think Mac would agree with you," Nybbas pointed out. "His anger and hatred are almost visible, and they aren't exactly befitting an angel. How long before his hatred causes him to fall from Heaven? A week, a month?"

Mac took a calm steadying breath and stepped forward. "Don't crow too soon. Now, since you obviously intend to force Alastor and Tristan to relive the past, let's get it over with right now."

Nybbas shrugged. "As you wish."

Mac barely caught Tristan as he tipped forward and collapsed to the floor in a deep sleep. Alastor had fallen back on the bed, also out for the count.

"You'll leave them alone after this." Mac picked Tristan up and placed him on the bed.

Nybbas merely vanished from the room.

Mac sat on the bed and held Tristan in his arms as his two lovers relived the past in their dreams.

Tristan shook violently and woke with a blood-curdling scream. Mac gathered him into his arms as his lover wept and clutched at his chest, as though searching for the gaping wound he still felt.

Across the mattress, Alastor slept on, the only sign of movement, the steady rise and fall of his chest.

Mac waited for his second lover to wake, but after nearly an hour had passed it became clear he wasn't going to do so any time soon.

Tristan eased himself out of Mac's embrace and crawled across to Alastor. "Alastor, wake up," he urged, giving him a light push. "Mac, what's wrong with him?"

Mac didn't know, but he joined Tristan next to Alastor to see why the demon wasn't waking up from the demonic sleep. "Nybbas," he shouted. "Get your arse back up here and explain yourself."

Nybbas appeared in the room with a scowl on his face and fury in his eyes. "How dare you summon me in such a manner? I don't answer to angels."

Mac bounded off the bed. "I don't care who you answer to. Why isn't Alastor waking up?"

"He'll wake when he's seen all he has to see of his past."

"Tristan woke up nearly an hour ago."

"Tristan died."

"What are we supposed to do, wait until Alastor has lived out his entire life? That could take years."

Tristan began to shake Alastor in earnest. "Damn it, wake up, Alastor. Wake up."

"He won't wake unless I allow him to," Nybbas pointed out with a bored yawn. "How did you enjoy your little journey through time, Tristan?"

Tristan glared at the demon. "I didn't. It was petty and spiteful. Hardly worthy of a demon at all."

"Coming from an incubus, that's laughable. *Your* only talent hangs between your legs. I have powers that can be used against anyone — human, demon or even angel."

Mac turned back to Alastor and pulled him into a sitting position. His hatred was forgotten for the moment as worry and concern took its place. "Come on, Alastor, wake up." Holding his hand over Alastor's heart, he concentrated all his focus on bringing Alastor round. "Come on, sweetheart. Wake up and tell me off for calling you pet names again."

Nybbas chuckled at his efforts. "His sleep is demonic in origin. The powers of a lesser angel like you are hardly a match for my own."

"Raphael," Mac shouted. Raphael, whom Mac suspected had been lingering around watching ever since he'd left, appeared straight away, along with Michael. "Can you wake him?"

Michael and Raphael both stepped forward. They each placed a hand on one of Alastor's shoulders and their auras began to glow with a blinding light. Alastor's eyes fluttered open and the archangels stepped back again.

"You don't play fair," Michael chided, as he turned to Nybbas.

"Calling in the archangels isn't exactly making it a level playing field," Nybbas countered. "Still, it makes no difference. There was little more for Alastor to see in his past, just more self-pity and regret, until he took his own life a few days after murdering Duach — or Tristan, if you prefer."

"I killed myself?" Alastor asked.

"And joined us in Hell shortly after. I'll no doubt see you there again soon." Nybbas smirked as he vanished from the room.

Raphael and Michael vanished a moment later.

"I'll be back in a minute," Mac said. "I just need to go have a word with Raphael about something."

"Is there a problem?" Tristan asked.

Mac shook his head and vanished from the room. He had to know why Raphael had encouraged him to see Alastor's past, when it was so obvious having the knowledge would destroy them.

* * * *

"You set me up," Mac shouted at Raphael, unheeding of the other angels and newly passed over humans milling around the area.

"I did nothing of the sort." Raphael's voice was calm. "You wanted to know what Alastor did in his past and now you do."

"You wanted me to see him as a killer, to ruin our relationship."

"He *is* a killer."

"He isn't the same man he was then."

"You're right," Raphael agreed. "He's worse now because he's a demon."

"He barely uses his powers."

"Only because you keep a close eye on him."

"You don't know that."

"It doesn't matter."

"I want to know how to fix this."

Raphael frowned at him. "Fix what?"

Mac raised his hands in frustration. "*This.* I want things to go back to how they were before. I want to forget what he did."

"You're asking me to remove the memory of what happened?"

"Yes."

"Request denied." Raphael folded his arms across his puffed out chest. "I have been telling you for years, Alastor is not to be trusted. Now you know why. If I remove the memory, I believe you'll return to his bed as before."

"How do you know I won't anyway?"

For the first time Raphael appeared unsure. "You wouldn't."

"I love him. Even knowing what he is and what he has done cannot change that. But I hate him as well."

"He's a demon. All he deserves is your hatred and contempt."

"Angels aren't supposed to hate anyone," Mac pointed out. "How can I be an angel with hatred eating up my soul?"

"By doing what you have to do, destroying the demon."

Mac backed up a pace. "I can't kill him. I'm a healer."

"You've killed demons before," Raphael reminded him.

"During the war, in the heat of battle," Mac argued. "This is different. It would be murder."

"He's a demon."

"I don't care. It's wrong and you know it."

Raphael looked about. "We seem to have drawn quite a crowd." He waved Mac to a quieter area. "Why does it bother you so much?"

"Because I love him."

"That's not what I meant. Angels and demons have been bitter enemies since time immemorial. Why does seeing him commit murder bother you?"

Mac opened his mouth to speak, but Raphael raised a hand to stop him. "Think about the question carefully before you answer."

Raphael lowered his hand and Mac gave the question a little more thought. His first instinct was to say witnessing anyone committing murder was a horrific thing to see. Then he realized he had seen people die on the battlefield many times. Why did seeing this one incident shake him to the core? In his heart he knew Tristan being the victim made the difference.

In all the time the three of them had been together, Alastor had shown Tristan nothing but love. To see one of his lovers with the blood of the other on his hands was something he'd never anticipated. If Alastor's place in Hell had been earned by killing anyone else, Mac knew he would be seeing things differently right now. He'd be taking Alastor in his arms and holding him while his lover came to terms with what he'd done. Only because the victim was Tristan did Mac stop himself from offering Alastor the comfort and assurances he craved.

"He doesn't deserve to be comforted," Mac muttered almost to himself.

Raphael smiled. "No, he doesn't."

Mac hadn't realized he had spoken so loudly. He scrambled to put the rest of his thoughts into words. "If he'd killed anyone except Tristan, I'd be okay with it."

"Okay with it?" Raphael's face clouded over with anger.

"Not okay," Mac hastened to amend. "But I'd be able to deal with it."

"No human's life has greater value than another. Each soul is equally precious."

"I know that, but it was Tristan."

Raphael placed a hand on his arm. "You know Tristan is your soulmate. But it shouldn't make a difference who Alastor killed."

"I know, yet it does. I can't look at Alastor without seeing him crouched over Tristan with blood on his hands."

"I'm not going to remove the memory of what he did. You will have to learn to live with it."

"Can you remove Alastor's and Tristan's memories of the past?"

"They need to learn to live with them too."

Mac sank onto the grassy floor. "How?" he whispered.

Raphael sat beside him and was quiet for so long Mac wondered if he had not heard the question.

"By letting Alastor go."

Mac didn't know if he could do that. Angry as he was, and repulsed by what he had seen, part of him still loved the demon. He was still contemplating Raphael's advice when Michael appeared in front of them. Raphael stood and greeted the other archangel.

"Raguel requests our presence for the vote," Michael said. With all that had happened, Mac had forgotten the petition of the archangel to forbid relationships between angels and demons.

Raphael indicated he'd also heard the summons.

"Will you join us?" Michael asked, as he reached down a hand to help Mac to his feet.

"It's rather irregular to allow a lower-ranked angel within the voting chamber," Raphael protested.

Michael gave him a smile. "But not forbidden. I think Machidiel should be allowed to see the vote."

Raphael frowned. "If you think his presence will sway my vote, you're very much mistaken."

Michael started to walk toward the chamber. "Since I don't know *officially* how you intend to vote, why would I hope to sway you at all?"

Mac followed the two archangels. They reached the chamber a few minutes later. Surprisingly, none of the other angels from the meeting at Michael's home appeared to be present.

Raphael left the two of them and stalked across the room to Raguel. Mac hovered at the edge of the chamber, unsure of where to go.

"You don't have to see the vote if you don't wish to," Michael assured him. "I thought you'd like to be here to see who votes which way. If I judged incorrectly, you are free to leave."

"I'll stay." Mac searched the room again, hoping to see some familiar faces from Michael's meeting. "Are the others here?"

"No, most of them await the decision outside the chamber or with their lovers." Michael led him over to the seating area and Mac found a place on a bench to wait. The chamber was small and Mac suspected he might have missed it completely if Michael and Raphael had not been guiding him there.

"Do you know which way the vote will go?" Mac asked.

"I'm afraid not, and your arguments with Raphael won't help sway his vote either."

"I'm sorry. Do you really think he'll vote to forbid relationships just because of what has happened between us?"

"We'll see. At least now you know why he's so set against the idea."

Mac supposed he couldn't blame Raphael. "Maybe it would be better if they vote to outlaw relationships between angels and demons. I've been wondering lately if maybe I'm not cut out to be an angel anymore."

"Are you sure you don't feel that way simply because you don't want to make the decision of what to do about Alastor?"

"Maybe that's a part of it," Mac admitted. "But Tristan is a demon too, and I would give up my wings to be with him in a heartbeat."

Michael opened his mouth as though he was about to say something, but Gabriel distracted him by calling the room to order. Michael went to take his own place with the other archangels, while Mac fidgeted in his seat.

Gabriel addressed the room at general, although there were relatively few angels present, just the archangels and maybe half a dozen others, including Mac. "We're here to vote on whether relationships between angels and demons should be forbidden."

Mac tried to catch Raphael's eye, but the archangel would not gaze in his direction.

With very little ceremony, the archangels cast their votes and Mac kept a mental tally of their decisions. There were fifteen archangels in total and the votes were seven against imposing the rule and six for it when it came to Raphael's turn.

"For," Raphael stated firmly, before finally meeting Mac's eyes. Mac ducked his head, but not before seeing the apology in his superior's expression. At least the decision had not been easy for him.

The final archangel to vote was Michael. Mac wondered if he would abstain from voting again, knowing his vote would be the one to make the difference.

Everyone in the room focused on Michael. Mac squirmed in his seat. The archangel's next words could alter his life forever. What would he do with the rest of his life if the law was imposed? He had already made the decision to give up his wings to be with his lovers if necessary. Even with what had happened with Alastor, Mac could not give up Tristan, which meant his decision stood. But how could he protect his lover without his powers?

"I abstain." Michael's words rang clear and Mac breathed a sigh of relief.

Mac remained seated as the archangels and the other observers dispersed. Raphael stalked past him without a word. Michael, on the other hand, lingered until the room had emptied and just the two of them remained.

Michael sat down beside Mac. "Well, it seems you are free to return to your men."

"Are you going to tell me why you always abstain from voting?"

"No." Michael's tone made it clear he would not elaborate further.

"Can I ask your advice about Alastor?"

"You may," Michael said, "although I cannot make your decision for you."

"I know. Did you know who Alastor had murdered?"

"Yes."

"Why didn't you tell me?"

"I'd hoped you wouldn't find out."

"Why?"

Michael sighed. "I knew it would tear the three of you apart. If Alastor were to lose your love completely, he could never be saved."

"What makes you think he hasn't already lost my love? He murdered Tristan."

"Love — true love — is not lost as easily as you think. If you didn't love Alastor, then the decision of whether or not to send him permanently back to Hell would be easy. He would have died at your hand as soon as you discovered his crime. You still love him."

Mac knew Michael was right. "How can I love the man who killed my lover?"

"With all your heart — or let him go."

"I don't know if I can do that."

Michael didn't ask him to clarify. "You should return to Earth, but before you go, I would remind you of something Raphael said to you a short while ago. Each soul is equally precious."

"I know I shouldn't let the fact it was Tristan who died influence me."

"That isn't what I meant. Alastor has a soul too."

Mac leaned forward and buried his head in his hands. Michael's hand rested on his shoulder and Mac felt calmness wash over him. He still remembered what Alastor had done, yet the memory didn't seem quite as sharp. He turned to Michael with open curiosity.

Michael smiled and raised a finger to his lips.

Mac nodded his understanding and thanks. Michael had taken his anger at Alastor and banished it. With hatred no longer blinding him, the decision of what to do didn't seem quite as daunting.

* * * *

Mac wasn't surprised to find Raphael waiting for him outside the chamber. He stood apart from the other angels who had gathered. Pel and Astra stood across the way. Metatron was with them, no doubt confirming the result of the vote. Even from across the crowd Mac heard Pel's 'yes' as he fist punched the air. Astra merely looked relieved. She gave a sharp nod and vanished from the realm, no doubt returning to her lover to convey the result.

Mac could tell Raphael was waiting for him to approach. He also knew he could not avoid speaking to his superior about what had happened inside the chamber. If he were to return immediately to Earth, it would no doubt result in Raphael following hot on his heels.

Resolving to take the bull by the horns, Mac approached Raphael, who led him into a nearby empty chamber.

"It seems you can return to your lovers after all," Raphael commented.

"No thanks to you," Mac snapped, forgetting in his anger he was talking to his superior and a powerful archangel. It seemed as though Michael had removed his fury at Alastor alone.

"You wrestle with the decision of what to do about your lovers," Raphael said. "Had the petition passed, the decision would have been made for you."

"I thought you encouraged free will?"

"We do."

"Yet you sought to remove mine by casting your vote."

"The problem of angels and demons forming relationships has been around for far longer than you and your lovers have been together. What makes you think this was just about you?"

"In the past you voted for such relationships to be allowed to continue."

Raphael's eyes widened for a moment. He was clearly startled by Mac's response and the angel wondered if he had said something he shouldn't have. Raphael recovered himself quickly.

"I see Michael has told you how I have previously voted."

"Yes, he did."

"He should not have done so."

"It's too late now. Does it bother you to know I'm well aware of the fact you only voted for the petition now because of me?"

Raphael frowned. "Yes, it does."

"Why? If you truly believe what you say, then why does my opinion matter?"

Raphael rubbed the back of his neck. Mac pressed on with his questions.

"Is it because you're supposed to be impartial and vote for the good of everyone? And this time you know you haven't?"

"I voted according to my conscience."

"You voted to part me from my lovers. At least have the courage to admit it."

Raphael stood silently for several long minutes. "Very well. I admit it. I wanted to take the decision out of your hands."

"Even though you know Tristan is the other half of my soul, you sought to separate us."

"Tristan is a demon now."

"I love him, and yet you still voted for the petition. By seeking to split me up from Alastor, you would have also parted me from Tristan."

"That can't be helped."

"Just so you know, I'd have given up my wings if the petition passed." Mac knew he would be wasting his time to argue any further and he turned to leave.

"One last thing before you go. If you truly meant what you said to Alastor about wanting him to leave, why does it bother you which way I voted?"

"Because you sought to separate me from Tristan as well."

"Is that the only reason?"

"Yes."

"Really? Or is it because maybe, despite everything he's done, you don't want to let him go?"

Mac disappeared back down to Earth rather than answer the question. Michael and Raphael had given him a lot to think about.

Chapter Sixteen

"You were gone a long time," Tristan commented when Mac returned.

Mac looked about the living room. "Where's Alastor?"

"He went for a walk."

Mac stuck his head through the bedroom door and saw Alastor's things were still there. At least he hadn't left them entirely in the lurch.

"What took you so long?" Tristan asked. "I thought you just wanted a quick word with Raphael about something?"

"I got distracted."

"By what?"

Now the petition was out of the way, Mac didn't see the point in keeping quiet about it any longer. "The archangels were voting on a petition to ban relationships between angels and demons. Michael invited me to see the outcome."

"What?" Tristan shot to his feet and his demon horns sprouted out of his head, evidence of his anger. "Why didn't I know about this? Did Alastor know?"

"No, Alastor didn't know. I didn't see the need to tell you both about it."

"You didn't think maybe I'd like to know there's a risk of losing you?"

"There was no risk."

"Then the angels voted unanimously to letting relationships continue?"

"No."

"Then there *was* a risk."

Mac pulled Tristan toward him and wrapped an arm round his shoulders. "You would not have lost me. I would have simply given up my wings to be with you."

"Oh."

Mac gave Tristan a peck on the lips. "Yes. So stop worrying."

"You'd really have given up being an angel for me?"

"Of course."

"What about Alastor?"

Mac froze and shifted from foot to foot.

"Mac?" Tristan prompted.

"I don't know," Mac said. "Before, I would have given up everything for him too, but now…"

"Alastor's still the same person."

"I know that, deep down I know, but I can't forget what he's done."

The soft footfall in the doorway drew their attention and Tristan saw Alastor had returned.

Silently, the demon disappeared into the bedroom, closing the door behind him.

Tristan followed Alastor into the bedroom and found him once again packing his suitcase.

"You aren't leaving? What about rescuing Cody?"

"I can't stay here with you and Mac. We all know I'm still jealous of what you and Mac have, just as I was in the past."

"It's strange, because I always thought it would be my jealousy issues that tore us all apart."

"You might get jealous, but you don't lose your temper over it. Until I can control my temper, you're both better off without me. Mac agrees with me."

"Don't speak for me," Mac interrupted as he joined them.

"You saw what I did," Alastor reminded him. "You said you'd kill me if you saw me again. Well, now's your chance. I won't fight you. You can do it without fear of repercussions. I'm a demon and you're an angel. It's your duty to rid the world of the likes of me."

"It's my duty to save you," Mac said.

"I'm past saving."

"No one is completely irredeemable," Tristan argued.

Mac wondered if Michael had worked some of his magic on Tristan as well, before he realized his young lover was simply the type of person who could forgive far easier than himself. Mac felt a brief pang of shame at himself, as well as pride in Tristan. He would have made a wonderfully compassionate angel were it not for him.

"I killed you!" Alastor shouted back. "Don't you understand yet? Your blood is on my hands."

Tristan took a deep breath. "I hadn't forgotten. I can still feel the pain of the blade sinking into my chest."

"All the more reason for me to leave."

"We need to stick together," Mac reminded him. "We still need to figure out a way to get Cody back to his own life and fighting amongst ourselves isn't going to help."

Alastor gave his reluctant agreement. "I'll stay until Cody is freed. I suppose one of you has a rescue plan? Because I've still got nothing."

"That's because you don't listen." Michael's voice echoed through the room. *"I see the time I spent with you at the pub was completely wasted."*

"What's he talking about?" Mac asked. "Since when have you and Michael been drinking buddies?"

"It was just once," Alastor said. "And I don't see what that's got to do with anything."

"Remember what I told you about Tristan's powers."

Alastor frowned for a moment, before Raphael's voice joined Michael's. *"You're crossing the line between guiding and actively assisting, Michael,"* he chided.

Then the two archangels became silent.

"What did he mean about my powers?" Tristan asked.

"Michael told me once you were very powerful because you drained Mac, an angel, of his powers."

"I was human at the time," Mac reminded them.

"According to Michael, that makes no difference."

"How does that help us with Cody?" Tristan asked.

"I think it's Michael's way of telling us you're powerful enough to rescue Cody from the Underworld."

"He's a prisoner of the Demon King, the most powerful of all demons."

"I know."

"Are you saying I'm more powerful than the Demon King himself?"

"Hallelujah," Michael muttered for them all to hear.

Alastor seemed thoughtful as he considered their options. "Come on, Tristan, let's go save Cody."

Tristan watched Alastor change swiftly into his demon form and, with a little concentrated effort, he soon did the same. Tristan hoped Alastor knew what he was doing.

"Come home safely." Mac kissed Tristan on the lips. Alastor turned away before Mac could do the same with him. They would have to talk more after Cody had been rescued and try to repair their damaged relationship.

"I promise," Tristan said before he and Alastor disappeared down to the Underworld.

* * * *

Tristan looked around the cavern they had arrived in and wondered what might be the best way to go about rescuing Cody. He and Alastor were just two low-ranked demons. How could they be expected to take on and defeat the most powerful demon of all?

"This is probably the archangels' way of ridding the world of two more demons and getting Mac back on side," Alastor muttered.

"You don't really believe that."

Alastor appeared resigned. "Come on—let's go see the Demon King."

"Can't we try and sneak in and get Cody out that way?" Tristan suggested.

"It won't work. Cody's his prisoner and the Demon King alone can release him."

"He won't do it willingly. Is there no other way?"

"Other than raising an army to defeat him, no."

Tristan trailed after Alastor, as they wove their way through the long, winding tunnels, each turn bringing them closer to the throne room and the moment when they would have to decide what they were going to do.

Inside the large cavern, demons congregated in small groups. The Demon King sat on his throne, surveying the various groups with a bored expression. It wasn't long before he spotted Tristan and Alastor lingering near the door. He waved them forward with a wide grin. "Have you decided to bring me another pet?" he asked, waving toward Cody, who sat on the steps of the dais. "This one spends most of his time sleeping."

"No," Alastor said. "We've come to bargain for Cody's release."

The Demon King laughed. "And what would you offer me in return?"

"Name your price," Tristan said quietly. "I'll pay it. I'll take his place if I have to."

"What use would I have for an impotent incubus?"

"What use do you have for a mortal?" Tristan countered. "He has no powers. He's of no value to you at all."

A hush fell over the crowd of demons in the room. Tristan guessed it wasn't often someone dared to argue with the leader. Alastor's gaze flitted between the Demon King and the other demons. Tristan had no doubt that if things turned nasty, the demons would turn on them before they betrayed their king.

The Demon King waved his hand and Cody screamed and clutched his head. His tormentor puffed out his chest and sighed in contentment.

"Oh shit," Alastor swore.

"*What is it?*" Tristan sent his thoughts directly to Alastor.

"*He feeds on pain and fear.*"

Tristan had suspected as much during his previous visit. *"You mean, like I feed on sex?"*

"Exactly. He can feed on Cody for eternity."

"What do you feed on?" Tristan asked.

"Whatever's in the fridge."

"That's not what I meant."

"I know. I get a power boost each time I use my powers to influence someone. My powers are a 'use them or lose them' kind of deal. The more I use them, the more potent they become. If I don't use them for a length of time, I have to start small and build them up again."

"Have you been using them much recently?"

"Not enough to influence the Demon King, if that's what you're thinking."

"What about his followers here?"

"One or two, perhaps, but I'm not powerful enough to take on them all."

The Demon King watched them calmly. "Are you finished your little chat?" he asked. "Except it's nearly dinner time and I'm rather bored with this discussion now."

Tristan took a step forward. "Name your price for Cody's release."

"He's not leaving the Underworld," the Demon King answered. "His place is here. Besides, I think you'll find he likes it here. Like you, he has found his pleasure in the bed of a demon. Nybbas has taken quite a liking to him."

Tristan tried to hide his surprise. "You know about Nybbas?"

"Of course. No one plays with my pet without my permission. Nybbas has been loyal to me for many years, and this is his reward."

Nybbas stood at the edge of the crowd. He didn't appear to be enjoying his reward. In fact, from the barely concealed glare on his face, he seemed rather pissed off, if Tristan wasn't mistaken. Maybe things weren't as much to the dream demon's liking as the Demon King imagined.

Suddenly a new voice spoke in Tristan's mind and he knew it was Nybbas. *"Cody does not want to return to his life."*

"How do you know?"

"We are lovers."

"Is that what he wants, or what you want?"

"It's what we both want," Nybbas stated. *"Will you help me free him?"*

"You have a plan?"

"I do now."

"And will you let Cody return to his own life if that is his choice?" Tristan asked.

"He'll choose to stay with me."

"But you'll give him the choice?"

"There's no choice for him to make," Nybbas insisted. *"He'll stay with me."*

"Unless it's his decision, I won't help you."

"He'll choose to stay with me," Nybbas repeated.

"Then why worry about giving him the option to choose?"

"Very well. Cody chooses. Will you help me?"

"Yes," Tristan agreed.

"Good. Now, here is what I want you to do…"

* * * *

Alastor could tell Tristan was communicating with someone, and while he suspected it might be Nybbas, he didn't know for sure. He was pretty sure the Demon King could also tell there were some secret discussions going on, but hoped he suspected they were between Alastor himself and Tristan.

Then, with no warning at all, Tristan launched himself up onto the throne and locked lips with the Demon King. Alastor stared at him in confusion.

Around the room, demons fell to the floor, dropping to sleep instantly as Nybbas worked his magic on them. Now that was one powerful demon. Alastor was glad he had switched sides, at least for the moment.

Nybbas stepped forward, whipped off his cloak, and placed it round Cody's shoulders, clearly staking his claim.

"So, you've just switched sides, have you?" Alastor asked. "After all you've done to us?"

"Cody deserved his revenge on you and Tristan for leaving him to his fate down here."

"We had no choice."

"Tristan is one hell of a powerful demon."

Alastor nudged a nearby sleeping demon with his hoof. She didn't stir. "So are you."

Nybbas shook his head. "There's no comparison. Tristan has always had the power to free Cody. He could free every demon in the Underworld if he chose to do so."

"He wouldn't do that."

"Of course he wouldn't." Nybbas fussed over his lover, ensuring he was modestly covered. "But he could have freed Cody long before now."

"He isn't free yet."

"He will be soon."

Alastor stared at the throne and cringed. "Is there any particular reason for Tristan slobbering all over him?"

"I needed a distraction?" Nybbas suggested.

"And that's the best you could come up with?"

Nybbas assisted Cody to his feet. "Tristan is an incubus."

"Do you think I don't know that already?"

Nybbas looked at him condescendingly. "When Tristan dominates, he feeds."

"I *know* this!"

"Did you know he doesn't need to fuck to feed?"

"What?" Alastor asked. "An incubus feeds through sex, everyone knows that."

"They feed through dominating sexually. Now, who would you say is in control at the moment?"

Alastor didn't need to see Tristan again to answer the question. "Are you telling me Tristan can feed through kissing?"

"If he dominates the kiss, then yes. Just as he can feed through fucking his lover in the mouth as easily as fucking him up the arse. As long as he is in charge, he can siphon power from the one he feeds off."

"Bloody hell!" Alastor watched Tristan and the Demon King. "Why doesn't he stop Tristan or take charge of things?"

"Because Tristan is stopping him," Nybbas explained. "The Demon King is frozen to the spot and the longer Tristan feeds from him, the stronger the incubus gets."

"I thought the incubi were amongst the weakest of the demons."

"Those who feed from humans are," Nybbas agreed, "but Tristan has a rather different diet, doesn't he?"

"Are you telling me Tristan is so powerful because of us?"

"That's *exactly* what I'm saying."

"Does he know?"

"He does now," Nybbas replied. "Watch."

Alastor looked to where Nybbas gestured. Tristan had finally pulled away from the Demon King, who appeared far from pleased.

"You dare to feed from *me*?" he snarled.

Tristan stepped back. Without a word, he reached down and a thick chain appeared, stretching from the Demon King's throne to Cody's ankle. With as much effort as it would take to tear a single sheet of paper, Tristan snapped the heavy chain, which evaporated under his touch.

The Demon King rose from his seat and let out a roar that echoed through the chamber. It was a testimony to Nybbas' own powers when not a single demon woke from the sleep he had placed them under.

"We're going to leave now," Tristan announced.

Alastor held out his hand for Tristan to take. Before Tristan could reach him, the Demon King launched himself off the throne. Tristan spun round and stopped the Demon King in his tracks with nothing more than a thought.

"You seem to have a handle on your powers," Alastor commented.

"I'm no longer rejecting them," Tristan said. "Like it or not, I'm a demon, and I'm not going to be pushed about by the biggest bully in the Underworld as though I'm nothing."

The Demon King broke free of Tristan's demonic hold. "You think you can take me on?" he shouted. "Armies have tried to defeat me and failed. Do you imagine *you* can do what an army can't?"

Tristan shook his head, but Alastor suspected it wasn't his answer to the question.

"It doesn't have to be this way," Tristan replied sadly. "Just sit back down on your throne and let us walk away."

The Demon King disappeared from his place in front of the throne and appeared a fraction of a second later blocking Tristan's path.

Alastor watched in stunned amazement as a glow began to emanate from his lover. The bright light surrounding Tristan was reminiscent of the aura that surrounded angels and he felt himself drawn to it. He wasn't alone. The Demon King reached out a hand toward the aura. The moment he touched the light, he realized his error. Screaming in horror, he tried to recoil from the almost heavenly glow, but he discovered his mistake too late. One minute he was there, the next he was gone, and a skeleton of naked bones tumbled to the floor.

"Tristan, what did you do?" Alastor was almost afraid to approach his lover, even though the bright light had disappeared the moment the Demon King had fallen.

"I don't know," Tristan said. When he turned to face Alastor, Tristan's expression was almost as horrified as the Demon King's had been. "I think we should get out of here."

Alastor agreed and he turned to Nybbas and Cody.

"Your place?" Nybbas asked.

Even though Alastor wasn't thrilled with the suggestion, he transported himself home, the others following close at his heels.

When Alastor arrived back in the apartment, he had to curb his first instinct, that being to throw himself into Mac's arms and hold on for dear life. The memory of how they had left things stopped him from giving into the desire.

"Where's Tristan?" Mac asked, as Alastor collapsed onto the sofa.

"He was right with us." Alastor looked round the apartment. "Maybe he misjudged the time again."

"You've been gone for several hours," Mac said. "Even if he has forgotten to return to the exact moment he left, like you have, he should be here with the rest of you."

Alastor cursed his own incompetence at returning. "I'll go see if he's still down there."

"Any time today," Mac muttered, as Alastor continued to sit on the couch.

"I'm trying." Worry crept into Alastor's voice. "I can't seem to get down there. Let me try something."

Within the blink of an eye Alastor moved himself from his place on the sofa and into the kitchen. He walked back through wondering why his powers had failed him. "I can teleport, but it's like the Underworld is locked. Nybbas, can you get down there?"

Nybbas closed his eyes for several minutes. He opened them and shook his head. "No."

"What does this mean?" Alastor asked. "I've never known this to happen before."

Nybbas sat on the sofa, pulling Cody, who clung to his arm, down with him. He took a deep breath and for the first time Alastor saw the dream demon in his human form. Ebony skinned with white-blond hair, Nybbas was as striking in his human form as he had been as a demon. "Wow," he breathed.

Cody chuckled and ran his hand over Nybbas' chest. "I think he's impressed," he commented.

Nybbas didn't seem bothered. "It matters not, my love. Now, all we can do is wait until the Underworld reopens."

"What do you mean?" Mac asked. "Isn't it always open down there?"

"Most of the time," Nybbas clarified. "But occasionally, usually when a new Demon King comes to power, it closes for a short while. No one knows why. But I'm not going to worry about it. It'll reopen soon enough. In the meantime, how about you fetch a demon a drink?"

Mac glared down at Nybbas. "Excuse me? You aren't a guest here and I'm not your waiter."

Nybbas smiled. "I'm not your enemy."

"I beg to differ."

"I'm not," Nybbas insisted. "I may have meddled in the minds of you and your lovers, but they don't seem to have suffered any lasting harm from my interference. You might even say I've done you a favor, since your relationship can only become stronger now you know the truth."

Alastor snorted and turned to leave the room. *Stronger? Destroyed it was more accurate.*

The case Alastor had been packing earlier still sat on the bed. He sat down beside it and put his head in his hands.

"Alastor, are you okay?" Mac asked from the doorway.

"I'm fine. It's Tristan you should be worrying about, isn't it?"

Mac sat down beside him and nudged him with his shoulder. "I'll worry about whoever I want, including you."

Alastor sighed. "Don't mess with my mind like this. It was bad enough when Nybbas was screwing with me. I don't need you playing mind games too."

"Is that what you think I'm doing?"

"Isn't it? You made it pretty clear you wanted nothing to do with me once Cody was safely rescued from the Underworld. He's sitting out there on our sofa, probably making out with Nybbas."

"I don't want you to leave."

"What's changed your mind?"

"I've spent the last few hours wondering what's going on down in the Underworld and worrying about the two of you. Despite everything, I still love you."

"I murdered Tristan."

"I know."

"I'd say I'm sorry a thousand times if it would help, but words are rather inadequate."

"Not if you mean them."

"You know I do."

"Then I forgive you."

"Is it really that easy?" Alastor chanced a glance at Mac, hardly daring to hope.

"I'm an angel—we're supposed to foster forgiveness. I can't remain an angel with hatred in my heart."

"You're a man as well, and the man hated me just a little while ago."

"I know, and I'm sorry for that. They do say love and hate are two sides of the same coin. I think I understand what the saying means now. As angry as I was, I can't stop loving you. You're pretty much stuck with me."

"Even though I'm a murderer?"

"It was a long time ago. You're a different person now and have been for a long time. I'm sure the Alastor I'm hopelessly in love with would undo what he did if he had the power to do so."

Alastor's tears spilled over. "I'm sorry. I'm so sorry."

Mac pulled him into his arms and held him as he sobbed. "It's going to be okay. I promise. We'll get through this, the three of us together. It was how it was always meant to be."

Alastor shook as Mac held and comforted him. Finally he drew in a shaky breath and sat back to meet Mac's eyes. "What if I do it again?" he whispered.

Mac didn't need to question what Alastor was talking about. "You won't kill. We won't let you."

"But you know how jealous I get. Even though I'm with you two, I can't seem to stop the green-eyed monster from rearing its ugly head."

Mac brushed Alastor's tears away and smiled. "I know you get jealous, but we're going to find a way to cure you of that."

"How?"

"By loving you so thoroughly and so completely, you won't have any cause for jealousy."

"You already do."

Mac rubbed his nose against Alastor's. "Yes, we do, but so far our relationship has been one drama after another. First Lawrence, then Tristan's transformation, then Cody and Nybbas. We've never really had the time to just be together, the three of us."

"Seems to me like Tristan should be a part of this discussion," Alastor commented. "Just because you're prepared to forgive me, doesn't mean he will."

"I suspect he's already forgiven you."

"You do?"

"Yes. Even though he's a demon right now, he was far more an angel than I."

"You really think we can get through this?"

"Yes, just as soon as Tristan returns we'll prove everyone wrong who doubts we can make this work. Can you travel down there yet?"

Alastor tried again, but the Underworld was still blocked. "No."

"I wonder if the archangels know about this," Mac said, which seemed to prompt the arrival of Raphael and Michael.

Raphael seemed annoyed to see Alastor in Mac's arms, but he declined to comment. Michael, on the other hand, appeared as serene as ever. "Good work, Alastor," he offered. "Cody is free now."

"He's in the clutches of Nybbas," Raphael pointed out.

"They are lovers," Michael amended. "Cody is able to leave if he chooses. He is no longer a prisoner. He stays with Nybbas because he wishes to."

Raphael didn't look convinced Cody had made the right choice, but declined to say anything further.

"And what of you, Machidiel?" Michael asked. "What is your choice?"

"I choose Alastor and Tristan," Mac answered without hesitation.

Raphael stared at him aghast. "Even knowing what Alastor did to Tristan?"

"I love Alastor. Maybe I wouldn't if I had known all along what he had done, but it's too late now."

"And what of Tristan? Do you think he'll want to share his bed with the man who took his life?"

"We'll discuss the matter when Tristan returns," Mac stated simply.

The two archangels exchanged a glance Alastor couldn't quite interpret.

"What is it?" Mac asked, clearly confused as well.

"Tristan can't return to you," Michael said.

Alastor didn't want to believe Michael's quiet declaration. "He'll come back as soon as the Underworld is unlocked."

"Tristan *can't* return," Michael repeated. "Even when the Underworld reopens, he will be unable to do so."

Mac turned to Alastor with a glare. "I thought you said Tristan was okay?"

Alastor shrank back from his lover. "He was. I swear it."

"He speaks the truth," Raphael grudgingly confirmed.

"Then why can't he return?" Mac asked.

"Tristan has been taken prisoner," Michael explained. "And freeing him will not be as easy as freeing Cody."

Alastor stood up and faced the archangel. "I don't accept that."

Michael shrugged. "Accept it or not, it's the truth. When the Underworld reopens you'll see for yourself."

Epilogue

Tristan had never seen a demon like the one who had appeared before him. He stood taller than even Machidiel, with strawberry blond hair falling to his shoulders in soft waves. Golden horns protruded from his head, although they were the only sign he was a demon. He was absolutely beautiful, so much so even Tristan's lovers paled in comparison. Tristan wondered why his form didn't appear to be repulsive like the rest of the demons.

"I see we have a new King." The stranger glanced at the skeletal remains of Demon King. He didn't seem overly concerned at the loss of the most powerful being in the Underworld.

Tristan tried again to return to the world above, but just as before, nothing happened.

The new demon chuckled. "It won't work."

Tristan didn't bother to ask how he knew what he was trying to do. "Who are you?"

The demon ignored him as he swept toward the throne, taking a seat easily, as though he had done so many times before. He caressed the bones of the arm of the throne as though he touched a lover. Tristan shivered as he imagined the newcomer touching him in such a way. With a crook of his finger a bone from the Demon King's skeleton flew across the room, lodging itself in one of the arms of the throne.

"You are a young demon, younger than any other king we've had. I don't think you'll last more than a decade."

"King? I'm not... I'm just... He..."

"The Demon King lies dead at your feet, and you will now take his place."

"What if I don't want the job?"

"That's your hard luck. You killed your predecessor, which means you're the new king, whether you like it or not. You have more power than you can ever dream of and dominion over all the demons of the Underworld, save for myself, of course."

"If I'm so powerful, why can't I leave?"

"Because the price you pay for your power is you are my prisoner here." The demon waved a hand and something glowed at the edge of Tristan's vision. He looked down and saw he had a manacle round his ankle and a chain stretching away from it, disappearing into the ground. It shone brightly for a moment more before disappearing from sight.

"Why?"

"It is part of the bargain I made with the archangels many centuries ago. They would not seek to destroy me providing I contained the most powerful of our kind here in the Underworld. Right now, that would appear to be you."

"There has to be other demons more powerful than me."

The demon gestured to the skeleton again. "Yet you have done what so many have failed to do."

"What if I refuse to be king?"

"Then another will kill you before the week is over. All you have to do is sit and wait."

Tristan didn't like the sound of that any more than the idea of being king. "Then I'm stuck down here, in this hideous form, for the rest of eternity?"

"Your form is quite unique."

"I hate it!"

The demon waved toward the wall behind the throne and a doorway appeared. "You'll find your chambers through there. Within them you can take whichever form you wish, as can any guest you invite there. And by that, I mean what *you* wish. If your guest wishes to visit as a human, you can force them to take demon form and vice versa. Your powers are greater now."

"What about you?" Tristan asked. "What's your role in all this?"

"I keep you from leaving the Underworld and waging war on the angels."

"I'd have thought you would be all for it."

"I lost my taste for war long ago. I can think of far more pleasurable ways to spend eternity."

"So you keep the peace while the rest of the demons fight amongst themselves for the throne. Do they know they become your prisoner when they finally get what they want?"

"No. If they knew, they'd stop fighting amongst themselves and turn their attention on the world above."

Tristan realized he would keep this strange demon's secret, just as the previous kings had done before him. He would not—could not—be responsible for unleashing hordes of demons on the unsuspecting human race. "Why has no other king let it be known he is a prisoner?"

The demon roared with laughter. "And let them all know he isn't the most powerful demon of all, as he professed to be when he claimed the throne?"

"I'd like to speak with Alastor," Tristan said.

"You may summon him if you wish. He will have no choice except to heed your command. I'll leave you to celebrate your new status with your lover."

"He's not my lover anymore."

"I'm sure he soon will be."

"Some celebration this will be," Tristan muttered. "And how the hell do I explain to him why I have to stay here?"

"I'm sure you'll think of something. But know this, I would advise you against telling him the truth or speaking of me."

Tristan snorted. "I don't even know who you are."

The demon stood up from the throne and glided closer. "Oh, I forgot to introduce myself. I'm The First Demon and known by many names." He leaned in to whisper into Tristan's ear. "You would probably know me as Lucifer."

Tristan gasped and shrank back. "The fallen angel?"

"Archangel," Lucifer corrected. "I see my reputation precedes me."

"But Alastor told me you were defeated and without powers. You're supposed to be a prisoner down here."

"As you can see, my powers are very much intact—and I am most certainly not a prisoner."

"But Mac said—" Tristan cut himself off as he realized he had inadvertently spoken Mac's name.

Lucifer smiled. "You can say his name if you wish. The ground won't open up and swallow you if you dare to speak the name of an angel. He is your lover, after all."

"Don't you mean *was* my lover?" Tristan asked. "I'm trapped down here and he's up there."

Lucifer ran a finger down Tristan's arm. "A long distance romance, unless you can persuade him to join you down here. If he cares for you as much as you seem to think, perhaps he'd consider joining us."

"He'd never do that!"

"Then if you wish to continue to share your bed with more than one person, you'll have to search elsewhere. That, however, is neither my concern or of any interest to me, unless you're offering yourself to me, in which case I might be persuaded."

Tristan shook his head, but didn't say a word. Was Lucifer actually flirting with him? He wasn't sure he wanted to know.

"Very well, if you'll excuse me, I have other business to attend to."

Tristan watched as Lucifer swept from the room. He had become a prisoner of the most famous demon of all. He needed his lovers with him, both of them, but not until he thought of something to explain why he couldn't return to their home. He trudged toward the entrance to his chambers, letting the rocks close behind him as he stepped inside.

Eternity in the Underworld stretched out before him. He'd tried to do the right thing. He'd struggled to be a good man and curb the sexual appetite of the incubus side of him. He felt as though his efforts had all been for nothing. Mac was lost to him and their ménage was broken.

Tristan felt for the first time since his arrival in the Underworld that he was truly in Hell.

About the Author

I live in England, in a quaint little village that time doesn't seem to have touched. No, wait a minute—that's the retirement biography. Right now I am in England in a medium sized town that no one has ever heard of, so I won't bore you with the details. Keeping me company are numerous sexy men. I just wish that they weren't all inside my head.

L.M. Brown loves to hear from readers. You can find her contact information, website details and author profile page at http://www.totallybound.com.

Totally Bound Publishing

www.ingramcontent.com/pod-product-compliance
Lightning Source LLC
Chambersburg PA
CBHW030131180626
46812CB00002B/652